The
Violent Season

THE
VIOLENT
SEASON

SARA WALTERS

sourcebooks
fire

Copyright © 2021 by Sara Walters
Cover and internal design © 2021 by Sourcebooks
Cover design by Maggie Edkins Willis
Cover images © Jakub Krechowicz/Shutterstock; Lana Veshta/Shutterstock; Jamen Percy/
  Shutterstock
Internal design by Michelle Mayhall/Sourcebooks

Sourcebooks and the colophon are registered trademarks of Sourcebooks.

All rights reserved. No part of this book may be reproduced in any form or by any
electronic or mechanical means including information storage and retrieval systems—
except in the case of brief quotations embodied in critical articles or reviews—without
permission in writing from its publisher, Sourcebooks.

The characters and events portrayed in this book are fictitious or are used fictitiously. Any
similarity to real persons, living or dead, is purely coincidental and not intended by the
author.

All brand names and product names used in this book are trademarks, registered trademarks, or trade names of their respective holders. Sourcebooks is not associated with any
product or vendor in this book.

Published by Sourcebooks Fire, an imprint of Sourcebooks
P.O. Box 4410, Naperville, Illinois 60567-4410
(630) 961-3900
sourcebooks.com

Library of Congress Cataloging-in-Publication Data

Names: Walters, Sara A., author.
Title: The violent season / Sara Walters.
Description: Naperville, Illinois : Sourcebooks Fire, [2021] | Audience:
  Ages 14. | Audience: Grades 10-12. | Summary: Wyatt Green is convinced
  that the annual spate of violence striking her small Vermont town is
  caused by a shared sickness, but she begins questioning her
  assumptions--and her memories about the night of her mother's murder--as
  she is drawn to her classmate Porter and away from her best friend Cash.
Identifiers: LCCN 2021023970 (print) | LCCN 2021023971 (ebook)
Subjects: CYAC: Murder--Fiction. | Violence--Fiction. | Grief--Fiction. |
  High schools--Fiction. | Schools--Fiction. | Vermont--Fiction. | LCGFT:
  Novels. | Thrillers (Fiction)
Classification: LCC PZ7.1.W3615 Vi 2021 (print) | LCC PZ7.1.W3615 (ebook)
  | DDC [Fic]--dc23
LC record available at https://lccn.loc.gov/2021023970
LC ebook record available at https://lccn.loc.gov/2021023971

Printed and bound in the United States of America.
VP 10 9 8 7 6 5 4 3 2 1

For Katelyn, and all our Novembers

The Violent Season depicts an unhealthy and abusive relationship. If you or someone you know needs help or information on this kind of relationship, visit **LoveIsRespect.org**.

1.

When Cash told me he wanted to kill Porter Dawes, we were standing on the peak of Lawson's Bluff, our sleeves pulled down over our hands. It was the first day of November, and winter already had Vermont in its fists. Below us, Wolf Ridge spread out like an open wound, a gash sliced through the mountains. We went up there to smoke the weed we had left from the weekend and to be away from town. Wolf Ridge had a way of closing in on us. The mountains crowded us. Finding higher ground was the only way we felt less suffocated.

I slid my lighter into my back pocket and crushed the last nub of the joint we'd been sharing. Cash stared at his feet, inching the tips of his shoes closer to the edge of the bluff.

"I mean it," Cash said. "I'll do it."

My skull felt too small for my brain. When I looked at Cash, it took a moment for my eyes to focus.

"Shut up, Cash."

He pulled a crumpled pack of smokes from his jacket pocket. Caught a filter between his lips. I handed him the lighter.

"I even know how I'd do it," he said, talking around the cigarette. He took a hard pull, the cherry lighting his face orange.

"Oh yeah?"

He nodded and said, "Would be messy, though."

"Messy?"

"Maybe too messy."

I tried to imagine it—Porter Dawes with all of his blood on the outside.

I knew better than to encourage Cash. The last time he'd gotten an idea like that and I'd played along, he'd ended up on probation. When I played along, he only got hungrier.

But I was hungry, too. He offered me his half-spent cigarette, and I took it, thinking of Porter Dawes in pieces.

"Messy how?" I asked. I rolled the cigarette filter between two fingers and watched him. I was always watching him. I was always waiting to see his face change, to see his lips move. I memorized every half smirk and every crease that gathered in his forehead when I said something wrong.

"Too bloody. Hard to clean up after."

It was already almost dark. Winter in Wolf Ridge meant making sure you were off the mountain before the sun dipped behind it. Before the cold wrapped itself around the town and pulled tight. My lips tingled with nicotine. My fingers were numb, but I felt warm. Somehow, I was certain I could feel Cash's warmth beside me. He burned and glowed like the lit end of my cigarette.

It took me a second, but I realized I was grinning. Grinning about Porter Dawes, insides on the outside, bright and red and angry.

It happened every November—the people in Wolf Ridge were suddenly overwhelmed with a hunger for violence. No one was sure why or when it started, but we were plagued and delighted by images and dreams of murdering strangers and friends and ourselves. Everyone knew it was real, but we all pretended it wasn't, just a boogeyman story you tell kids to keep them from getting in trouble when they're older. Our parents lied to us and said it was an urban legend, but we all knew they dreamed about slitting their own parents' throats. We all knew.

As if it were a sickness, some kind of seasonal virus like the flu, there were those of us who ended up coming down with it harder than others. Cash was pretty much patient zero this year. I could almost see his urges radiating off of him.

"Why Porter, though?" I dropped the cigarette and stubbed it out with the toe of my shoe.

Cash slid his hands into his pockets. I could see his cheeks were turning pink, cold-bitten. It was getting darker. We needed to leave.

"Because he deserves it the most." Cash watched the city below us. The streetlights were popping on in rows.

I didn't know what Porter Dawes had done to make Cash mad. But it was November, so it could have been nothing. It could have been that Porter looked at him wrong. Our November Sickness had infected Cash to his core. He must have carried the virus from birth, sleeping inside him, but now it was awake. And it was hungry.

I looked over my shoulder at the car, parked a few yards back, behind the DEAD END sign nailed to the fence blocking the rest of the dirt road. The fence was new. Last November, Kristen Daniels smashed through the old one in her dad's truck. I remembered my pulse quickening when the news made its way through the school hallways. My mouth watering. Cash skipped school that day and came up here to see the crime scene tape laced through the tree limbs, to peek over the edge of the bluff and see the mangled remains of the truck at the bottom. It took them days to remove it. A few of us stood along the tree line smoking cigarettes as they brought the crane in to lift it out of the twisting branches and underbrush. There was a constellation of blood splatter across the spiderwebbed windshield.

Cash's hands were still tucked into his pockets. I wanted to slide my fingers around his wrist, inch my hand between his arm and hip bone. I didn't. I looked down at Wolf Ridge, watched the headlights moving down Getty Street. Sometimes I could see my house from the bluff, but that night, it was too dark. The lights must have all been off. No one was home.

"Maybe I'll just burn the whole place down." Cash flicked the lighter on.

Even in the glow of the flame, his eyes still looked black.

2.

No one was home when I got to my house. Cash dropped me off, and I shuffled across the cold-burnt lawn with my hands shoved deep into my jacket pockets. He was on his way to a shift at the diner, the only restaurant in Wolf Ridge that stayed open past eight. If you wanted the chain places, you had to take the interstate a good fifteen miles into the city. We hardly ever did.

I pushed the door shut behind me with my foot, dropping my backpack on the floor. The house was quiet. Only the small lamp in the living room was on. Dad left it on for me when he was going to be late—just one of our many unspoken codes. As I moved through the house, I flicked lights on. Being there alone in the dark made me anxious. When Dad got home, he'd probably make a joke about the electric bill.

He taught history at the high school, but with all the budget cuts, he'd also had to pick up some extra tutoring jobs over in the city. Most people in Wolf Ridge had to go into the city to find better jobs. During the day, the streets in town were practically empty. Our little blip on the map was quiet most of the time. There was one stoplight in the whole place, and Cash and I liked to lie in the middle of the road underneath it when he got off late shifts at the diner. The road was so quiet at that hour that we could hear the click of the stoplight changing from green to yellow to red.

I turned the corner into the kitchen and flipped the light on, heard it pop to life overhead. The fluorescent buzz lit up the mess on the countertops—half-drunk mugs of coffee, the pile of unwashed dishes in the sink, crumbs from microwaved breakfast sandwiches eaten in a hurry. Dad's favorite mug was beside the sink, stained with a dried drip of coffee down one side. I'd painted it for him when I was three or four and my grandma took me to one of those pottery studios in the city. *Wyatt loves Daddy* was written messily across it in bright purple paint, with pink hearts filling up the rest of the empty porcelain space.

The magnetic whiteboard on the fridge had my dad's slanted handwriting scrawled across it. *Wy—home late, leftovers in fridge.* I wrinkled my nose at the idea of congealed spaghetti and opted for the pint of banana chocolate chip ice cream in the freezer, grabbing a spoon from the drawer. Even though I was headed upstairs to my room, I left all the lights on downstairs.

I checked the front door twice—pulled hard on the handle, made sure the bolt was in place. Some people in Wolf Ridge never locked their doors. We were not those people.

The stairs squeaked as I walked up them, and I gave little more than a sideways glance to the photos that lined the wall. It was more like a shrine than a display. All of the mismatched frames were occupied by photos of my mother. A summer afternoon at the edge of the river, grinning as she watched my dress billow out on the rope swing. Christmas morning in that old purple robe, coffee in one hand, toddler me wrapped up in the other arm, all of her dark brown hair piled on top of her head. The lace of her wedding gown, and that bright, goofy smile on my young father's face. I didn't look at them because if I did, I'd have to remember that they were the only place I'd ever see her again.

I hurried up the rest of the steps, urgently reaching for the light switch at the top. In the dark, I felt the same sensation as always—something cold and wet on the carpet soaking into my socks. A puddle of black at the top of the staircase. The faint outline of a smeared handprint on the wall.

My hand was shaking by the time it found the switch. The light came on, and the carpet was dry again. The wall was clean. Another photo of my mother grinned brightly at me from a simple brown frame.

In my bedroom, I was free of her gaze. There were no photos of her in here. I'd taken them all out—plucked the photo booth strips from my mirror, replaced the photo in the frame on my bedside table with one of Cash and me at the lake that summer. I could erase her from my room, at least, even though my dad wallpapered the rest of the house with her memory. In here, I could pretend she still existed outside of framed photos and a few boxes of clothes out in the garage. In here, I could shut the door to all the ghosts that filled our house. Even as empty as it was, it felt crowded.

Dad would be home by ten, and at midnight, Cash would get off work and wait for me outside. He would get a bottle of something with his fake ID and park his car on the next street over from mine. We would walk out past the high school and climb up into the bleachers by the football field and drink, and Cash would eventually get drunk enough to let me kiss him. When we were sober, we pretended I wasn't in love with him. It was easier for both of us that way.

My dad would fall asleep on the couch watching sports highlights, and when I came in the front door at four a.m., he'd wake up and see me, but he wouldn't ask me where I'd been. Sometimes, he'd make a joke like, "Ah, I knew I had a daughter." And I'd lean over the back of the couch and kiss the top of his head and trudge up the stairs to my room, ignoring the Mom Shrine in my peripheral vision. For my dad, the whole house was a shrine. The whole town. All of Vermont.

It was barely after six, but it was pitch black outside my bedroom window. I pulled the curtains closed, keeping all that darkness out of my warmly lit room. The pint of ice cream was sweating in my hand, and I set it on my night table, the spoon clattering down beside it. I wasn't hungry anymore. I crawled under my blankets, still in my clothes, wishing my dad would come home, or that time would speed up and Cash would get off work.

When I was home alone, it was just me and the ghosts. They were everywhere. One in a worn-out purple bathrobe. One in a wedding dress trimmed with lace. One chasing an unruly toddler around the upstairs hallway, their laughter and footsteps so loud sometimes I could barely sleep. Most of them were harmless. Most of them smiled at me when I saw them, even opened up their arms, offering to hold me. But there was one I was afraid of. It stood at the top of the steps some nights. Walked up and down the hall to my dad's door and back, steps dragging over the carpet. This one seemed to show up the most when I was home alone. I stared at my closed door and pulled my covers tighter around myself.

I remembered an evening last year when I'd come home past curfew yet again. My mother had stayed up waiting for me, and as I kicked off my shoes in the foyer, she appeared in the hallway from the living room. I watched her slowly fold her arms over her chest, and I knew she was probably vacillating between anger and trying to be gentle—lately, her irritation unleashed something in me that wanted to cut into her with curse words and promises to disappear. I think by then she was scared of what I might do to myself in a backward attempt to hurt her.

It was always Cash who made her confront me. He was always the reason her daughter came home late, smelling of smoke and his cologne. She was my mother, and she wanted me safely behind locked doors once the streetlights came on. But I was sixteen, and I wanted Cash. I wanted to lie in the middle of the football field smoking with him until all my limbs went heavy and I could pretend for a moment that we were somewhere else. Alone together, anywhere but there.

That night, I swayed a little as I got my second shoe off, the high still thick in my head. She watched me, face fixed in a frown, but one that looked more sad than angry.

"Wyatt," she started, and my shoulders fell. Her frown seemed to deepen.

"Are you happy with the choices you're making?"

I didn't know why I was always so ready to rip her to shreds just for loving me. I didn't see love; I saw control. I saw her laying another brick in the wall she wanted to build between Cash and me. And I hated her for it.

I let out a laugh. Started up the stairs.

"Who fucking cares, Mom?"

I spent so much time wishing for her to leave me alone, to let me destroy myself in peace. Later, I wished for just one more night of her waiting for me, wanting me to love myself more than I loved a hand grenade in the shape of a boy.

When the front door opened and closed, I suddenly jolted awake, unaware I had even fallen asleep. My body ached from being curled up so tightly, my knuckles white and stiff from clutching my blankets. I uncurled myself, releasing my grip on the blankets and pulling them down. The clock on my bedside table read 9:33—it was Dad getting home from the city. The pint of ice cream I'd brought upstairs sat in a puddle of water, the cardboard soggy. I rubbed my eyes, trying to wake up, listening for more sounds from my dad downstairs. But it was quiet. I picked up the wilted ice cream container and walked to my door, opening it and moving out into the hallway. The lights were all still on.

I stood at the top of the steps, listening, but I still couldn't hear anything. From where I stood I could see the front door, and the bolt was pointing up, unlocked. I swallowed the sudden clench of unease in my throat.

"Dad?" I called down the steps.

Nothing.

"Dad, is that you?"

The door that led out to the garage creaked open loudly, the sound startling me so much that I gasped, jumping back from the edge of the top step and into the wall behind me. I wanted to call out again, but my voice was stuck in the sharp, sudden panic that had formed in the center of my chest. Footsteps moved from the garage door into the kitchen. My jaw clenched, and my eyes locked on the bottom of the stairs, waiting to see who emerged into the foyer. Maybe it wasn't Dad. Maybe it was one of those fucking ghosts, unlocking and opening doors, taking another hard stab at my sanity.

The footsteps got closer. I was starting to shake with fear and panic. I was losing it—I knew I was. I was just hearing things. Seeing things. Ghosts. Unlocked doors.

A set of wide shoulders turned the corner from the foyer and stood at the bottom of the steps. There was my dad—his messy dark hair, salt-and-pepper stubble, and the sudden glow of his straight, white grin.

I let out a breath I didn't realize I was holding.

"You scared the shit out of me." The words came out of my mouth in a rush of air. "I called for you."

"Sorry, honey," he said, leaning on the end of the railing. "I was taking the trash out to the garage." I must have looked irritated, because he laughed. "It's just me, Wyatt."

I started down the steps, giving him a light shove as I went past him at the bottom. He chuckled and followed me into the kitchen, where I tossed the cardboard ice cream container into the sink along with the spoon.

Dad started looking through the cabinets, twisting up his face. He towered over me at six feet and change. His presence alone felt safe, protective. His hair stuck out wildly in a few places, and his unshaven face made him look a little older and even more tired than usual. He had on his black-framed glasses, but he still squinted into each cabinet he opened. I leaned against the counter and watched him, one eyebrow raised. I never said so, but the quiet moments we shared were the ones I loved the most. He didn't expect anything from me—I didn't have to talk about Cash, or the fact that all my coats on the hooks by the front door were steeped in the scents of weed and cigarettes. In those moments, I got to just be the little kid who'd made that mug for him.

He gave up on looking through the cabinets and picked up the mug, stepping around me to rinse it in the sink. He set it back on the counter and got to work putting on a pot of coffee, despite the fact that it was nearly ten. Dad could drink shots of espresso and still pass out twenty minutes later in front of the TV.

He noticed me studying him and lifted his eyebrows as he spooned coffee grounds into a clean filter. "Do I have something on my face?" he asked, smiling.

"Just that neck beard you're working on." I folded my arms. He grinned and ran his fingers over the stubble on his chin.

"What, you don't like it?"

I tried to look unamused, but he had this habit of making me smile, just exuding goofiness and an ever-present wide, glowing grin. I couldn't help but let myself smile back at him.

"You look like an old man."

"I am an old man."

"Oh, bull."

In the time we'd been on our own, we'd developed our own language. If he could get me to tease him, could get me to smile a little, he felt reassured, and we didn't have to talk about anything serious. It was when I didn't return his jabs, when he came home and I stayed in my bedroom, that he gave me his best serious face and asked what was wrong.

Right then, though, we were both okay. Coffee was brewing and Dad was grinning at me and I was rolling my eyes at him and we were both okay. We didn't have to talk about the ghosts that night.

Mom watched us from a photo taped to the fridge. The kitchen smelled like coffee, and Dad reached up to the top shelf of the pantry to pull down the stash of cookies he thought was secret, but definitely wasn't.

"Coffee and cookies?" he offered, the cookie package crinkling as he shoved one hand inside. "I'll even let you have the last macadamia nut."

"Nah, I think I'll go let Cash feed me bad diner food." I pushed off from the counter, and before I could walk past, he leaned down in front of me, offering one stubbly cheek. I wrinkled my nose at him but gave his cheek a kiss anyway.

"Do you want a ride over there? It's getting cold." Dad spoke around a mouthful of cookie.

"I'm good. A little fresh air won't kill me."

I stopped at the front door to bundle up—sweater, jacket, beanie. I pulled my ankle boots on and tugged my socks up over the bottoms of my jeans. I could feel my dad peeking around the corner at me. I knew he wanted to ask me to stay home. I knew he wanted to tell me he hated when I was out late with Cash. But my dad was already too full of pain and grief. There was no room left in his body for another ounce of negative emotion.

As I grabbed my keys from the hook by the door, I heard the ghosts upstairs.

One of them was crying.

3.

Last November

I remember it was cold. It had snowed most of the afternoon. The ground was covered in a few inches of fresh powder that crunched softly underfoot. The plows hadn't even come through the neighborhood yet, so my street was slippery and thick with dirty slush. I carved out a path of footprints on my way down the block from Getty Street. It was the first big snow of the season. We'd had a flurry or two, but this was heavy, and it stuck to the streets.

Cash and I had spent the afternoon at his house, smoking downstairs, watching the snow pile up in front of the tiny basement windows. I remember he dragged me outside at one point, both of us in T-shirts and jeans, our bare arms immediately prickling with goose bumps. And for no reason at all, we stood out in the backyard, snowflakes sticking to our hair, all bloodshot eyes and bliss, and Cash kissed me on the lips, soft as a whisper, so tenderly that even a year later, I was sure I'd dreamed it.

I could tell someone was home when the house came into view. The front window poured yellow light out onto the snow-covered lawn. Mom's car was in the driveway. She worked as a nurse at the hospital, and I figured she was probably getting ready for a night shift.

The cold was biting at my face and hands, which I shoved deep into my pockets, searching for my house key. I wrapped my fingers around the chain I kept it on, the one my mom had given me when I was ten and started walking home from school by myself.

I was pulling the key from my pocket when I got to the front walk and realized the door wasn't locked. It was open. Cracked just a few inches, enough that a trickle of snow got swept inside each time the breeze blew toward the house.

I stopped a few feet from the door. Every sense in my body told me to turn around and run.

Four Novembers Ago

Ms. Linney didn't show up one Tuesday. We sat in the class-room alone for half an hour before the principal arrived. The room was so quiet. Like somehow we all knew.

Principal Harris explained that a sub would be there soon, and as she hurried to put on a video, her hands shook a little.

Later, we found out Ms. Linney was in police custody after her two toddlers drowned in the bathtub the night before. The newspaper said the investigation was ongoing but that the police didn't believe the kids' deaths were accidental. Only days later, Ms. Linney confessed to holding their heads underwater.

The day after, some of the other teachers stood in the hallway before homeroom and cried.

4.

If you really wanted to, you could walk the length of Wolf Ridge in less than an hour. Getty Street is the main throughway, running from the nature reserve at the north end of town all the way down to the interstate at the south end. My house sat near the intersection of Wicker and Getty, just a few blocks from the diner where Cash worked.

I met Cash the same way pretty much everyone in Wolf Ridge meets—as kids on the playground. Wolf Ridge isn't one of those towns that attracts a lot of new residents. Cash's dad and my dad were friends as kids, but strangely enough, our mothers both came from somewhere else. I think that's what made them both so interesting to everyone in town— they were outsiders. Cash's mom showed up in Wolf Ridge when she started high school, and mine arrived shortly after that. My mom's parents sent her to Wolf Ridge to live with her grandparents when they fell on hard times financially, and she met my dad and ended up staying longer than she'd planned. Cash's mom, on the other hand, bounced from foster home to foster home around our county until she landed with Cash's grandparents in Wolf Ridge and finally stayed put.

Cash and I thought this was why both our mothers had died—they weren't from Wolf Ridge. The town consumed them and spat them out. It was one of the reasons we'd been drawn to each other—we had always felt like outsiders. Our twin feeling of being foreign in the place we'd spent our entire lives became the invisible string that held us together.

The diner wasn't so much a diner as a bar that also served diner food. Wolf Ridge was so small that it didn't have enough people to warrant very many restaurants or bars, so ours were squished into one old building with a flickering neon sign on the front that simply read OPEN. The place had no name, but everyone in town just called it the diner or Watson's, since it had been owned by one member of the Watson family or another since it opened some forty years ago.

My favorite thing about the diner was the old jukebox that sat in the back corner. Over the years, some newer music had been added, making for a strange mix when it went on shuffle. It would jump from Johnny Cash to The Smiths to Hozier to Ray LaMontagne. My mom would always put a quarter in and play "Asleep" by The Smiths, even though my dad complained that it was too sad and slow to listen to during dinner. But I loved it. My mom would give me sips of her white chocolate milkshakes and pull me against her side and sing the words into my hair.

By the time I got to the diner tonight, my hands and face were pink and cold. I pulled off my beanie as I stepped inside, unbuttoning my jacket and looking around for Cash. The diner was basically dead, aside from a few regulars parked at the bar. Oasis was playing on the jukebox—"Champagne Supernova." I knew Cash must have chosen it.

I hung my jacket on one of the hooks by the door just as Cash emerged from the kitchen, drying his hands on the dirty white apron tied around his waist.

"Leftovers night?" he asked when he saw me, already grabbing a glass to fill with ginger ale for me.

I nodded and slid into a seat at the counter across from him. He added a splash of grenadine to the ginger ale, dropped a maraschino cherry on top of the ice, and slid it over to me.

"Grilled cheese? Milkshake?" Everything about us was routine and easy, but still, it filled my rib cage with warmth when he knew what I wanted without even asking.

"Grilled cheese. With provolone. And a tom—"

"A tomato slice, I know." He waved a hand at me as he disappeared through the kitchen door.

Cash was tall and slim—he had an inch or two on my dad, even. He wore his hair buzzed close on one side while a wave of dirty blond fell down over the other side, touching his eyelashes. He was always tossing it back in quick little flips.

His face was angular, his cheekbones high and his jaw strong. He was, by any standard, beautiful. But to me, Cash had been beautiful even before he'd actually become beautiful.

I remembered the summer it happened. We were fourteen going on fifteen. Cash sprouted up a foot, and his skin cleared, and he grew his hair longer, and suddenly—almost overnight, it seemed—he went from child to man. He looked different down to the bones in his hands, his lithe fingers no longer stubby or scabbed from playing outside in the woods. But even when he was small and mischievous and always had dirt under his fingernails, I had loved him. I had been enamored with Cash since grade school, a fact that we had fought over periodically ever since. I wanted to be with him, and Cash wanted to get out of Wolf Ridge. Actually, he wanted to disappear. He wanted to get far, far away, where no one knew who he was. He said he was afraid to be with me in Wolf Ridge. He was afraid of what could happen to me here. To us.

I watched him cooking through the order window. He flipped his hair back from his eyes and moved around the kitchen as smoothly as a dancer, like every move was choreographed.

Cash brought a plate out to me and set it on the counter. While I ate my sandwich, he wiped tables and put away clean glasses, ran the mop over the floor, and put dirty dishes into the bus bins. He made us a white chocolate milkshake, and we passed it back and forth, complaining about the upcoming calculus test and wishing our fall break would hurry up and arrive so we could drive up to Montreal and get out of Wolf Ridge for a few days.

Everything was simple and routine and familiar. Cash flipping his hair back, bussing my dishes, and finishing off the last of our milkshake. And me, turning in slow circles on my bar stool, quietly singing along to the songs that came on the jukebox. We found safety in the repetition of our days. At least if they were monotonous, it meant nothing catastrophic had happened. It meant there hadn't been blood or sirens or goodbyes.

But even in the safety of our familiar motions, Cash seemed tense tonight. He couldn't stand still. He paced as he spoke, tying and untying the knot on his apron, drumming rhythms on the countertop with his fingertips. Something had him on edge. I was picking up his energy like an electric current radiating from his limbs.

"What is it?" I finally asked him when he had been quiet for a few moments. The jukebox clicked and whirred as it moved to another record. The door on the bar side of the diner opened and closed as a few regulars came in. But I kept my eyes on Cash. When he looked at me, I could practically see fire burning in his eyes.

"What? I'm fine."

I just kept staring at him, shaking my head slowly. "No, you're not."

Cash turned and looked at the clock that hung on the wall behind him. He had twenty minutes left in his shift, but he untied his apron and hung it up behind the counter. Nate, the guy who always tended the liquor bar on the other side of the diner, gave Cash a nod and a wave, silently letting him off the hook for the night.

Before I could ask him what was going on, Cash had me by the wrist, pulling me out of the diner. I grabbed my coat on the way out the door, practically jogging to keep up with his quick, long steps. Something was under his skin; I could swear I saw it crawling up his bare neck, could feel it seeping into me from his hand on my wrist. He let go of me so I could climb into the passenger side of his truck.

Cash got in and started the truck but left it in park. He just stared at the steering wheel, his hands at ten and two, and I could tell his pulse was racing by his strangely quick breaths. The clock on the dash read 11:43, lighting Cash's face in its green glow.

After another long minute of silence, I reached over to him. I wrapped my fingers around his wrist and pulled one of his hands from the wheel to hold it between both of mine.

"What is this about?" I asked him, keeping my voice quiet, almost afraid to disturb the silence.

He let me hold his hand. Usually he pulled away, but he let me touch him. I kept studying him, waiting, watching his Adam's apple jump as he swallowed.

"Listen," he began, still not looking at me. "I heard something the other day. And I don't know if it's true, and I don't know if I can trust the person I heard it from, but I've been trying to decide whether or not to tell you."

Now it was me with the racing pulse. My heartbeat spiked hard against my rib cage. My throat suddenly burned with urgency and fear.

"What is it?" I asked.

Cash finally looked at me. I was squeezing his hand, and he let me.

"Nate had me take a dinner order over to the police station yesterday. When I dropped it off, the sheriff was talking to that detective—you know, the one from the city, what's his name, Daniels?—and as I was walking the food back to the conference room, I could hear them..."

When he trailed off, I leaned in, as if he had just started speaking more softly. He looked away from me, and I watched him wet his lips.

"Cash." I loosened my hold on his hand. "What?"

He stared at the steering wheel for another moment, and I could tell that he was trying to figure out the right way to say whatever it was. I let go of his hand in frustration.

"Cash, what the hell?"

He reached out and grabbed my hand again, and I was suddenly silenced. He rarely reached for me. I couldn't decide if I should feel soothed or even more fearful.

"They were talking about your mom."

The air inside Cash's truck felt thin and scarce. The breath I pulled in barely filled my lungs. He kept hold of my hand.

"My mom?" I managed to sputter.

Cash nodded, took in a deep breath, and sighed it softly

out. His grip on my hand tightened when he noticed I was
starting to pull it away.

"I think they have a new suspect. I think they might know."

Everything slowed down. We lost gravity. I drifted upward,
out of the truck, out of the parking lot, out of Wolf Ridge.
I watched the town from over the mountains, saw the lights
going out one by one until the green glow of the clock in the
truck was all that was left.

5.

Last November

I stood there clutching my house key for what felt like decades. Snow blew in steady waves into the crack in the door. Music was coming from inside the house—a song I didn't recognize. Something old and haunting that seemed to echo through the walls and out into the yard. I don't know how long I stood there staring at the door, but it was long enough for the song to end and begin again. It sounded like it was coming from the old record player in the living room where the my mom played her old vinyl that she kept in a crate in the den.

The song had reached the chorus again by the time I moved closer to the door. The November cold bit at the backs of my bare hands. I lifted one and pushed the door open farther, scanning the foyer for any signs of movement, listened for any sounds besides the music drifting in from the living room.

"Mom?"

I turned back to check the driveway again—there was her car. She was home. Maybe the wind had blown the door open and she hadn't noticed. Maybe she was in the kitchen, swaying to her music and boiling water for hot chocolate that we would share while she got ready for work. She'd take my hand and twirl me around and sing to me. She'd hold my face in her warm hands and kiss my forehead.

I tried again, louder.

"Mom!"

Maybe the music had drowned me out. I stepped inside, looking around. The song played on, the record crackling a little.

I hung up my scarf. Coat. Hat. Pushed off my ankle boots and left them by the door. I peeked around the corner into the kitchen but found it empty. The sink dripped quietly. Rhythmically.

I looked up the stairs. They dissolved into darkness halfway up, no lights on in the hallway.

"Mom? Are you in the shower?"

I started up the steps, taking them slowly, waiting for a response. Still nothing. No running water. No creaking floorboards. No doors swinging open. No sudden burst of her scent—jasmine soap and that cool, sweet perfume she wore.

Silence. Stillness. Darkness.

I was two stairs from the top, my eyes adjusting to the dark as I reached for the light switch on the wall.

That's when I stepped in it—something cold and wet. It seeped into my socks. I grappled for the light switch, trying to step somewhere dry. The hallway light popped on.

A hard gasp shook my lungs, and I had to grab the railing to keep from tumbling down the steps. My shoulder bumped two pictures off the wall, sending them into a noisy collision with the stairs.

The top step was black-red. Soaked.

One desperate red handprint ornamented the wall, right below the framed photo of my mother and me from three Christmases ago.

6.

Cash took a long drink from the bottle of maple whiskey he'd bought with his fake ID when we'd finally left the diner parking lot. The cashier at the liquor store, Bobby, always sold to Cash, even though he knew Cash was only eighteen. In Wolf Ridge, everyone pretty much knew each other, by face if not by name. Bobby knew Cash was Cash Peters, not Richard Doyle, like it said on the ID he used. But he never turned him away.

I had waited in the car while Cash got the booze, running everything over: the cops had a new suspect in my mom's murder, and Cash didn't know who it was, but he'd heard them say they were going to bring him in for questioning. *Him*—it was a guy. And if they were bringing *him* in, he lived here.

Even after we'd parked Cash's truck and walked the few blocks to the back gate of the high school football field, I was still running faces through my mind like a lineup. I was making a mental lineup of every face and name I knew in Wolf Ridge, trying to decide which person was most likely to have killed my mom. But the problem with Wolf Ridge was that *anyone* could have been a suspect. Especially in November, when the sickness peaked.

"I really don't think it has anything to do with being sick, Wyatt." Cash passed me the bottle. "It's more likely that it's just people killing other people."

"And themselves? Every November? Just one giant decades-long fucking coincidence?" I took an angry swig and shoved the bottle back at him. The liquor burned the back of my throat just as angrily as I'd thrown it back. I thought Cash of all people would believe the November sickness was real. He'd been here for all those bloody Novembers. He'd stood beside me behind the yellow police tape while the coroner pulled the body of that third-grade kid out of the river a few years back. Held my hand while we sat through another don't-kill-yourself seminar at school after that senior shot himself in the parking lot our freshman year. Read the paper with me at the diner counter the day after that guy from the city was found dead in his car at the edge of town.

I saw the hunger in him. I knew he felt it.

"I don't know. You want something to blame for what happened. Everyone does. But even if there were something like that going on, the person who killed your mom didn't do it because of some urban legend."

I didn't want to hear what Cash was saying. Because there had to be an explanation for why people drove their trucks off Lawson's Bluff. Or walked into someone's house and killed them for no reason other than *wanting to*. We did it because Wolf Ridge made us. Whispered it to us as we fell asleep. Carved its demands into our bones when we were born so that we grew around them, molded to fit.

I reached into Cash's jacket pocket and pulled a cigarette from his pack. I held it between two fingers, rolling the filter back and forth, not lighting up.

"What made your mom do it, then?" I knew immediately after I asked it that I shouldn't have. I wished I could pull the words back into my mouth. Instead, I put the cigarette between my lips and lit it. Cash sniffled in the cold, elbows resting on his knees, maple whiskey breaths coming out of his parted lips in warm clouds. He just nodded slowly for a few seconds, almost like he was saying *Yes, that hurt.*

When he didn't speak after another painful moment, I tried to backpedal.

"Cash, I—"

"I think she did it because she was sad, Wyatt." He looked straight ahead, out across the football field. "Sometimes people are just sad. Sometimes there's really nothing else to blame."

I took a long pull on my cigarette, if only to keep my foot out of my mouth. I was trying not to think about Cash's mom, with her pretty blond hair and her polite little laugh and the tiny diamond wedding band she wore, but I couldn't help it. I had never told Cash this, but I had dreams about what she must have looked like, wrists opened up, bleeding into her lap in the bathtub. I remembered Cash's father filling the bathtub with boxes and using it as storage for months and months afterward. All of the boxes held his mother's things. A bathtub tomb.

There was nothing pretty about what had happened to our mothers. There was nothing peaceful or beautiful or gentle about their deaths. We got older, and Cash started to drink, and I started to smoke, and we both found ways to explain what had happened to us, to them, ways that helped us sleep. I just needed him to see what I saw, to tell me he believed me. I needed him to validate me, because that was the only way things felt true anymore.

I held my cigarette between my fingers and reached out with my free hand to snatch the bottle from Cash. I wasn't going to let the entire night sink into silence, like it tended to when we talked about our dead mothers. I took a gulp, wincing at the sick sweetness that filled my mouth before I could swallow it. Enough of the bottle was gone for me to know that Cash was at least tipsy, on his way to drunk. I hadn't drunk as much as he had, but I didn't need to. I would kiss him sober. I would offer the skin under my clothes without coaxing.

I handed the bottle back to him. Put my cigarette between my lips again. Pulled my phone from my back pocket and turned on music, holding down the volume button until it was all the way up. I picked a song that sounded like the way I felt when I was close to him—a song that swayed with me and had a warm, bright beat and a pretty-girl voice singing about kissing on street corners and dancing in gold light.

I stood up on the bleachers and moved my hips to the music, lifting my arms, cigarette smoke swirling above my head. I looked at Cash, and I could practically see what he was thinking about reflected in his eyes: blood in a bathtub, holding me while I sobbed over my mother until I threw up in his backyard. Once someone brought up dead mothers, it was hard to dance that heaviness away. I took a final pull from my cigarette and stubbed it out on the cold metal of the bleachers. I removed the bottle from Cash's hands and set it aside, taking its place in his lap. I moved one knee on either side of his body and sank into him, winding my arms around his neck, curling my fingers into his hair. He tilted his head back to look up at me, studying me in the dim moonlight. I reached down for his hands and put them on my hips, urging him to hold me. I needed him to.

When I kissed him, he tasted syrupy sweet and liquor sharp. I held his face, pressed my lips into his, tried to urge him to hand over the weight he was carrying. I always wanted to save him from it, even if it meant my insides felt filled with lead. I leaned over him, took a handful of his hair to tilt his head back farther, exposing his throat so I could drag my lips down over it. He held me weakly, and I heard him let out a small sigh as I caught his skin lightly between my teeth. I wanted a reaction—anything. I just wanted him to do something, even if it hurt me.

"Cash." I sat back in his lap. I let go of his hair and pushed it gently back from his eyes instead, resting a hand on either side of his face.

"Why do you do this to yourself?" he whispered. The music had ended, and we were left with just the creaks of the old bleachers with each hard shove of wind. One gust blew my long hair over my face, and Cash pushed it back. He wrapped his fingers around my small wrists and stared up into my eyes.

Normally, I was all cuss words and cigarette smoke. Normally, I was rock-solid. With Cash, I was an eroded river-bank. With him, I found the one surface hard enough to chip away at me.

"Because I love you," I whispered to him. It came out in a broken little whimper, and I immediately felt ashamed, embar-rassed by how easily he broke me without even trying. That wasn't who I was.

Cash was shaking his head, pulling my hands away from his face so he could hold them between his own. He breathed warm air onto my cold fingers and rubbed them gently.

"You shouldn't." He held my fingers to his lips and touched a light kiss to their tips.

And I curled up in his lap, and he wrapped me up in his coat and his arms, and I buried my face in his neck, and we stayed there that way until it got later and colder and my breaths came out in shivers.

Three Novembers Ago

BOTCHED ROBBERY ENDS IN TRAGEDY

Wolf Ridge—Roy Baker, forty-seven, was shot and killed in a botched robbery attempt in Wolf Ridge on Thursday night. Baker was finishing his shift at Watson's Diner when a man entered, armed with a pistol, and demanded money from the register. Security camera footage showed Baker attempting to comply when the armed intruder suddenly fired his weapon, shooting Baker in the chest. The intruder fled the scene in an early model black Ford truck. Mr. Baker was pronounced dead at the scene.

Police are looking for any information regarding the robbery and shooting.

7.

Wolf Ridge High School had a student body of just 327. Some of the kids were from the next town over, one even more isolated than Wolf Ridge, if that was even possible. I'd known most of the kids in my year since we were in preschool. We'd made our friends in elementary school and stuck with them ever since, for the most part. In a small town, social status was difficult to shift or change, especially in the obnoxious politics of high school.

I'd been friends with Cash forever, but before I completely latched on to him our freshman year, I more or less floated between groups, finding a home wherever one was offered. The girlfriends I'd had growing up abandoned me when we got to high school, when I started to care less about boys and more about just one boy, that hopeless case of a boy that

I was determined to love until it killed us both. I think my need weighed on them, made me too heavy to be around. Sophomore year, when Cash's mom died, just about everyone but him disappeared for me.

Now, school was just busy hallways full of people I knew but who were, at the same time, ghosts to me. Feeling foreign in a place I'd lived all my life bred a deeper kind of loneliness than I'd ever known, and I wanted to blame it on everyone but myself.

I sometimes rode to school with Dad, since he taught there, but sometimes I insisted that Cash pick me up. On those cold November mornings, I always sought out the warmth of Cash's passenger seat, the two of us lingering in his car until the second bell echoed across the parking lot.

I was huddled down in my seat that Monday morning, knees to my chest, window cracked to let out the smoke from the cigarette we were sharing.

"What a fucking tool," Cash spat from the driver's seat. I looked up to see Porter Dawes weaving through the cars in the lot, tossing his backpack onto one shoulder. He wasn't as tall as Cash but was still tall, and he had a lean, muscular figure with biceps that filled out the sleeves of a white T-shirt. It couldn't have been more than thirty degrees outside, and he was hustling into the building without a coat on, laughing with a few other guys from the track team. He was pretty—clean shaven, in slim-fitting black jeans hung low on his hips. A tousle of caramel hair that he swept back with a push of his fingers.

The group disappeared through the front doors of the school, and I heard Cash grumble.

"The hell is your problem with Porter Dawes?" I asked him, cigarette smoke leaving my mouth with my words. I opened the passenger door, dropped the cigarette on the pavement, and stubbed it out with the toe of my boot.

"He's just a dick." Cash got out of the car and reached into the truck bed for his backpack. He hooked one strap over his shoulder, and the two of us moved briskly across the parking lot. I took two small steps for every one of his. I grabbed a handful of his jacket and pulled, just to slow him down.

Cash had never especially liked Porter Dawes. Porter was the golden boy at our school, the foil to how Cash saw himself in the social hierarchy. Even so, I knew there was something Cash wasn't telling me about Porter, about why he was so pissed at him, but I didn't press it. Our mornings were sacred. Gas station coffee, cigarettes, holding his elbow on the way inside. For that short walk from the truck to the school, I got to be his.

"Slow down, will you? I don't have your giant stilt legs."

Cash stopped suddenly and bent down in front of me. I grinned and shouldered my bag, leaping onto his back and wrapping my limbs around him. He hooked his hands under my thighs and jogged through the rest of the lot while I pressed my face into his neck, at home in the sweet morning scent of his skin. Cedarwood. Bergamot oil. The aftershave he'd used since freshman year.

And then he let me down when we made it to the door. And suddenly we were two separate people again.

Mr. Vaughn was the AP literature teacher at Wolf Ridge High. He drove in from two towns over every day, and I envied him his distance from Wolf Ridge. He went to some big university down in Connecticut, according to the diploma that hung on the wall behind his desk. He had just moved to Wolf Ridge the summer before, fresh out of that fancy university. During the first few weeks of school, I'd tried to guess how old he was—twenty-four? twenty-five?—but to most of the girls, it didn't really matter. All that mattered to them was that he wasn't from Wolf Ridge and that he had the conventionally attractive face of someone you might see in an underwear ad. But being from somewhere other than Wolf Ridge might have been enough for them all on its own. People from out of town were fascinating and exotic. I saw them as doomed, though. And Mr. Vaughn was no exception to the rule.

Mr. Vaughn had vintage movie posters on the walls of his classroom. *Casablanca. The Seven Year Itch. It Happened One Night.* He had a powder-blue suitcase Victrola on a side table and a crate of old records underneath—The Who, Pink Floyd, Prince, Billy Joel, David Bowie, Michael Jackson. He'd put a record on when we worked on essays or did group work, and sometimes I'd catch him swaying to the music as he walked around the room, hands in his pockets.

Quinn salivated over Mr. Vaughn the most. She was the only close girlfriend I had. Quinn had the kind of bright blond hair and pretty face that nineties pop songs were written about. She wasn't rail thin or five ten, but that didn't matter much to the guys in Wolf Ridge—Quinn was, for lack of a better word, *hot*. She was gorgeous in that effortless way that made most girls hate her on sight in that shitty way girls do. If I hadn't met her when she was a round-faced ten-year-old offering me a snack cake on the playground, I might have hated her too. Quinn was the one of the few remnants of my old life, one memento I had let myself keep. Since we'd met in grade school, she'd been a constant. When her parents divorced in sixth grade, she started spending weekends with her dad in Burlington, so we coveted our weekends together in Wolf Ridge. Those unforgettable moments—the every-other-weekend sleepovers and day trips to the lake in the summer—made her the best friend I'd ever had. As we got older, she was the only soul I shared anything with about Cash and, eventually, about my mother. As different as we were, being with her was one of the few places that felt like home. That felt safe.

When I dropped rather ungracefully into my seat in Mr. Vaughn's class that morning, Quinn whipped around in her chair in front of me, a sudden swing of blond hair and a pair of sea-green eyes on me.

"Wyatt. Look. At. Him," she whispered, eyes widening.

I lifted an eyebrow and turned my unamused gaze to Mr. Vaughn, who was sitting on his desk in black jeans and a long-sleeved, cashmere V-neck sweater. The collar of his white undershirt peeked out from underneath. To me, he looked young. Ready for this town to chew him up and spit him out as something worse.

I looked back at Quinn, shrugging and shaking my head. She looked offended at my lack of interest.

"God. You're a mutant. I don't know how you can look at him and not melt."

I couldn't help but smile a little. Quinn reached for my hands and grabbed them tightly.

"I forgot to ask you. What happened this weekend?"

I wet my lips. Quinn was the only person who knew about my strange, pathetic, endless need for Cash. Whenever I went an entire weekend without talking to her, she assumed he was the reason.

"Nothing happened this weekend."

"Yeah, okay." She rolled her eyes.

"It really didn't."

The late bell rang. Mr. Vaughn looked up to catch the last few people running in the classroom door.

"You know what, Wy? It's about four years past the time you should have let that shit go. So, let. That. Shit. Go." Quinn punctuated her words with little pinches along my arms, and I squirmed and slapped her hands away.

Something *had* happened that weekend, but not between Cash and me. I just didn't want to tell Quinn about my mom's case. I wanted to keep it to myself, at least until we knew more. I'd spent the weekend alone in my room, scanning old yearbooks and looking through the town's geotags online, creating a kind of catalog of the people in Wolf Ridge. When Cash had walked me home on Friday night, he'd said, "Please don't get obsessive about this," and even though I'd told him I wouldn't, I was already obsessed. I was weaving stories and putting together the events of the night she died—exactly what that therapist in the city had told me *not* to do. I was glad I didn't see her anymore.

"All right, settle down. Let's get started." Mr. Vaughn was walking around his desk to the whiteboard. He picked up a bright blue marker and wrote *Group Project* in big, slanted letters. The room collectively groaned.

"Yeah, yeah—your lives are so hard." Mr. Vaughn chuckled and capped the marker, turning to face us. I slumped into my seat, reaching out to touch Quinn's blond ponytail, twirling it around my fingers. I wasn't worried. Quinn and I always worked together on group projects. She pretended to help, and I did the bulk of the work. We had a system, so I tuned him out. I was back inside my mental catalog, running through my list of suspects again—a list Mr. Vaughn was on. Even his easy smile and unassuming looks weren't enough to make me trust him. Being a teacher at Wolf Ridge High, he knew my dad, and therefore he had met my mom more than once at faculty holiday parties and potlucks. He was less of a stranger than he felt like.

"With a partner, you'll pick a scene from one of the books we've covered this semester, write a script, and either film it or perform it live in class before winter break."

My head lolled against the back of my chair, an audible sigh escaping me.

"Don't worry, Wyatt," Mr. Vaughn said. "I'll make it a little more interesting for you."

I lifted my head and looked at him, both eyebrows lifted, waiting.

"I'm going to pick your partners for you."

The room erupted in more groans and whispers. Quinn turned around in her seat again and grabbed my hand.

"I like him less now," she whispered harshly, digging her fingers into the back of my hand. I smirked at her and patted her hand with my free one.

"You'll be okay. You may have to actually do some work, though."

Quinn flipped her middle finger at me as she turned back around. I gave her ponytail a little tug and smiled, pushing myself up straighter in my seat. I glanced around the room, trying to decide if I'd be all that horrified to end up partnered with any of the other people in the class. My eyes landed on one particular person.

"Porter," Mr. Vaughn started, looking at a piece of paper in his hand. "You'll be with Wyatt."

Porter looked at me and caught me staring, and my cheeks flushed, tingling with heat. I quickly looked away.

Quinn got partnered with James Lorey, and I heard her mumble "Fuck" under her breath. James had been infatuated with Quinn all year. I looked over at him and saw him grinning wildly, throwing up finger guns at Quinn, who mouthed *fuck you* at him.

Mr. Vaughn folded up his list of names. "All right, take the rest of class today to meet with your partner and pick what scene you'd like to use for your project. I want your decisions before you leave today!"

I could feel Porter's eyes on me from the other side of the room. I leaned over my desk and grabbed Quinn's shoulders, pulling her back so my lips were beside her ear.

"Twenty bucks says James gets to second by the end of this project."

Quinn gasped and jumped to her feet. I grinned and sank back into my chair, flinching and guarding myself with both arms, waiting for her to take a playful swing at me.

"Shut up, idiot. Go do some *Romeo and Juliet* scene with Porter Dawes," she muttered, giving my shoulder a little shove as she went past me, reluctantly shuffling over to sit beside James.

I made a face at her over my shoulder.

"So, uh—"

A voice startled me, and I whirled around. Porter was standing beside my desk, holding his books.

"Did you wanna pick something?"

My cheeks filled with heat again, and this time he must have noticed, because he smiled at me, which only made my face burn more. Porter turned Quinn's desk around and sat down facing me. I hadn't been that close to him...ever. Had he always had those impossibly long eyelashes? Those brown eyes that had hints of gold in them? With him so close, I could smell his—cologne? Aftershave? It almost smelled like Cash's. Close to it, at least.

I'd taken far longer than the appropriate amount of time just staring at him in silence, so I sat up straighter and shook my head a little. "Yeah, I guess so. Got anything in mind?"

"Well, as long as it's not anything from that terrible James Joyce novel..."

I smiled, then wet my lips and pressed them together, trying to wipe my expression clean. I hated when people could easily read me. I was cuss words and cigarettes, after all. Diamond tough. I didn't giggle and sweat over pretty boys like Porter Dawes. Besides, Cash seemed to hate him for some reason, so I mentally promised to resist whatever charms he had. Resist, resist, resist.

"Yeah, not really a James Joyce fan, either." I drummed my fingers on the desk, glancing back over my shoulder at Quinn. She was playing on her phone while James talked animatedly.

I must have been trying too hard to seem bored and disengaged, because Porter lifted both eyebrows and sat back in his chair a little, suddenly looking annoyed with me.

"What did I even *do* to you?"

The sharp irritation in his voice cut into me. I really had no idea how to respond. He must have done *something* to make Cash mad at the mere sight of him. I opened my mouth to answer, then closed it again, giving him a shrug instead.

"Nothing." I shook my head. "I just usually work with Quinn."

He didn't look convinced.

"I doubt that." He leaned forward again, his annoyance still plain. "This is about Cash Peters, isn't it?"

My pulse jumped at the mention of Cash's name, particularly because it came from Porter's mouth. I had a strange tendency to get uncomfortable when other people talked about him.

"What about Cash Peters?" I asked.

"You're like, together, aren't you?"

My chest got tighter and tighter. And then came the sharp sting of having to say, "No. We're just friends."

"Oh. Seemed like you guys were a thing. Figured you'd know that he hates me. Thought that might be why you're acting all squirrelly about being partnered with me."

"Squirrelly? I'm not acting squirrelly." Yes, I was. Still, I folded my arms defensively over my chest.

"Whatever you say. Do you wanna pick a book?"

"Why does Cash hate you?"

"What, you don't know?"

I felt an irrational wave of offense, like he'd just pointed out that I wasn't as close to Cash as I thought I was. Like he'd just told me I knew nothing about Cash. Maybe there was some truth to that.

"He's not much for gossiping." I snapped. "We don't really talk about people at school. Not our thing." A half lie, but Porter didn't need to know.

"Well, I think I know why, but I could be wrong. Who knows with that guy."

I was starting to hate Porter Dawes, too.

"Cash wouldn't hate you for no reason," I said, trying to keep the volume of my voice in check.

"Then it's probably because he thinks I did something that I didn't do."

"Okay. Cryptic."

Porter shook his head. "Can we just pick a book?"

I studied him warily, my mind running through possibilities of what Cash could think he'd done.

"Fine. What about *Gatsby*?" It was the only book I'd really liked that semester.

"Fine." Porter shrugged. "Any scene in particular?"

I considered my favorite scenes, and all of them involved Gatsby and Daisy having some heart-wrenching exchange. I chewed my lip, regretting my choice of book.

"I don't know, one of the parties? Could be interesting."

"Difficult to do with two people."

"Vaughn didn't say we had to be the only ones in it, just that we had to write it and shoot it, right?"

"Yeah, I guess so."

"So let's throw a party."

Porter let out a little laugh, then frowned when I didn't laugh with him.

"Wait, you're serious?"

I shrugged. "Why not?"

He considered this, watching me. I watched him back. Behind me, I heard Quinn say a sharp "Shut *up*" to James.

"All right," Porter said, sitting back in his seat. He never took his eyes off of me. He started to smile, and it made me squirm. "Let's throw a party."

8.

I found Cash by his locker after school. I found him there most afternoons if I wanted to ride home with him. He was switching out his textbooks, trading a calculus book for a copy of *The Great Gatsby*. I felt heat in my neck at the sight of the book, thinking of Porter and our project.

I swallowed that thought back, unsure why I was keeping it a secret.

"Hey," I said. "You got homework?"

Despite his general air of disinterest, Cash cared about school. School, he always said, was his ticket out of Wolf Ridge. Out of Vermont. His face was turned toward his locker, but I could still make out every feature. Every line and curve. I'd memorized them. I'd loved him in so many different shades since we were two sets of small hands building a castle in the playground sandbox. First, that innocent, unknowing love, which eventually turned all-consuming once I learned what his hands felt like holding mine, noticed the way he softened the most when he looked at me. I'd loved him like a brother, like a best friend, like a lover, like a caretaker—I'd learned to love Cash in every way I could, as if I knew I'd have to pick one version eventually, even if it wasn't the one I wanted.

"Nah, not really. Just some reading." He looked at me, and a smile pulled at one side of his mouth.

I would have asked more, but his eyes on me always derailed every train of thought I had.

"You wanna get out of here?" he asked after a beat of silence.

"Yeah." I watched him as he shut his locker. "Can you drop me off at home?"

He shook his head, shouldering his backpack.

"I've got a better idea."

On the way out to his truck, I fell into step beside him, two of my steps for every one of his. I followed him dutifully, unquestioning, the silence he offered me somehow enough.

When we reached his truck, he opened the passenger door for me and lingered beside it as I got in, his eyes on me.

"We're getting out of this stupid town for a little while."

Part of me wanted to argue, to get out of the truck and push him away, walk home, make him spend the afternoon alone. To make him think he didn't run my life, that he was just another person in the world instead of the only one.

But he was looking at me so hopefully, and his eyes were brighter than they'd been in weeks, and his spontaneous excitement was contagious, turning on a light inside my chest that had been dark for a long time. There was a key to it, and Cash held that key.

So I nodded, melted into the passenger seat, and we rolled the windows down and let the icy November air in like an old friend we'd picked up along the way, and outside, Wolf Ridge slid by in flashes of houses and street signs, bursts of laughter as we passed kids walking home from school. Outside his house, Cash left the engine running while we filled the truck bed with blankets and pillows, and then we took off toward the highway, screaming at the top of our lungs when we passed the THANKS FOR VISITING WOLF RIDGE sign. I swear even God heard us.

We took the highway to the turnoff for the lake and followed it until we felt like we were far enough away from absolutely everything. Until I noticed Cash's shoulders start to sink back, his grip on the steering wheel loosen, his jaw relax from its tight, clenched position. He pulled off onto the dirt road that led to our favorite spot. We parked a few yards from where the ground gave way to water, and Cash turned on the mix we'd made specifically for lying by the lake—all acoustic guitars and piano ballads and soft voices. The lake was our quiet place. It was where we went to feel like we were the only people left in the world.

We arranged the pillows and blankets in the truck bed and

collapsed into them. And without my prodding, without me asking, without me scooting closer and pushing my body into his arms, Cash reached for me. He pulled me against him, let me lay my head on his chest, and I felt him drag his fingers along my back. It was rare for Cash to show affection without a few gulps of something strong in him. He was terrified of getting too close to me, to anyone. But I knew I scared him the most. I scared him because I loved him so ferociously, so patiently, and he was always trying to hand my heart back to me, like a little kid scared to be tasked with carrying something fragile. Breakable. It didn't matter how much I promised I trusted him with it. He didn't trust himself.

But sometimes, he let me in just a little.

On the drive out, I'd wanted to ask Cash about Porter, about what he had done. I had worried, though, that bringing him up might sour the warm, sweet atmosphere we were building around us. I had wanted to stay safe inside of it with Cash. I'd wanted to leave Porter back in Wolf Ridge. Porter and his cheekbones and eyelashes and white T-shirt.

I sank into the scent of cedarwood and bergamot, lightened from the wear of the day, but still familiar and comforting. Safe.

"I'm applying to schools in New York." Cash spoke into my hair. I tilted my head back to look at him.

"New York?" There was that tightening around my rib cage again. I pushed myself up onto my elbow, looking down at him.

"You know I can't stick around here. I've always said I was going to leave for college."

He was right. He *had* always said that. Still, hearing him talk about it as a reality instead of some hope for the future made my insides twist with anxiety.

"Yeah." It was all I could get out. I pressed my lips together, looking at him. Cash. My Cash. But at the same time, he had never been mine. Would never be.

"Hey. C'mere."

Cash pulled me back down against his chest, his fingers tangling gently into my hair as he brought our faces closer together, his nose brushing mine. I wanted to cry. His sober tenderness was so rare, such a delicacy, that it almost always broke me into shards.

"You could come. You could get out of here, too. You know that," Cash said, trying to soothe me.

I tried to stay stone-faced. I tried to ignore the sweetness of his breath on my lips when he spoke. I shut my eyes so I wouldn't have to see the softness in his.

"You don't want me to," I whispered. "You don't want me with you. You don't want me. Once you leave Wolf Ridge, you won't need me anymore."

Cash silenced me with a hard, desperate kiss. He tightened his fingers in my hair, held my face to his, parted my lips with his tongue, and urged me onto my back. He'd never been so hungry for me, had never been the one to take control, to call the shots. It was always me, pathetic and needy, practically begging him to have me. And as much as I wanted to revel in it, to melt into the feeling of him wanting me, I could only think of the fact that he hadn't denied anything I'd said. He didn't want me to come with him to New York. He didn't want me at all—or he wouldn't once he was free of Wolf Ridge, at least. All I would be was a constant reminder of where he had come from and what he was trying to escape. Even if he loved me, I was still forever damaged by Wolf Ridge. Me, with my dead mother, just like his. Me, with the darkness I carried in the center of my chest.

But I let him have me. I pushed my jeans down, and he pulled my hair back so he could kiss my throat. It got colder, and our breaths came out in clouds, and my skin felt uncomfortably damp and warm and cold all at once as we moved. His muscles tensed and flexed under my palms, the sharp drag of my fingernails along his spine. I opened my eyes to watch him, to see his face change, lips parted and jaw slack, breaths uneven.

He was beautiful, but I could see him breaking. I could see his seams coming apart, his threads loosening. And even as he was right there with me, touching me, kissing me, taking me, he was already gone. He was somewhere in New York, crossing a plaza at some beautiful university with books tucked under one arm and a brightness about him that he would never exude for me, about me. And there was already a girl, though he didn't know her yet, and she was already the safety he had spent his life in Wolf Ridge searching for. And I was already lost—something he left behind to collect dust in the attic of his memory.

But I was too tired to feel the ache of it anymore. Needing

him was exhausting. I'd been trying to scale the walls around him for so long that I was starting to forget why I was still climbing.

We didn't say a word from the time we redressed and got back in the truck cab to the time he dropped me off. There was a new heaviness between us. Even his hands on me had felt like pity, like a goodbye he hadn't wanted to admit to out loud. I'd never felt so empty after giving myself to him, so hollowed out. But I'd been the one to offer myself up, to scrape out what was left of me and hand it over to him willingly, like he might be able to fill me back up with something better.

I walked inside and up to my bedroom, feeling the warmth of his touch under my sweatshirt turning cold, burning my skin until all I could do was tear off my clothes and sit on the floor of the shower while the water ran, trying to rid myself of him. Or really, to rid myself of my need for him. I was Sisyphus, and needing Cash was the stone I rolled up the mountain day in and day out, always expecting a different outcome when I reached the top but forever watching him slip away from me all over again.

For once, I just wanted to let him fall.

––––––––

Five Novembers Ago

A little kid out fishing in the river with his dad found her. It was early November, autumn still hanging on by threads, the last leaves still falling. I imagine they crunched under his feet along the riverbank as he ran, little fishing pole in hand, searching for the best spot to cast.

She was somewhere on the south bank, probably half hidden by cattails and underbrush. I imagine the little boy saw the white of her fingertips first, reaching out so delicately, a doll left to sleep in the weeds.

The paper said she was naked. The death was ruled a drowning. They even said she likely drowned much farther upriver and drifted down to Wolf Ridge, but I thought they were just passing the blame, trying to shift a bit of darkness off the shoulders of our town. They offered no explanation for her nakedness, for her lack of identity—just a drowning, just a body, just another November.

She stayed a ghost, someone's daughter without a name, laid to rest in a pine box. They buried her in the Wolf Ridge cemetery with just a cross to mark her grave. Every so often, the city news station did a story on her, showing an artist's rendering of her face, asking for information. But no one ever claimed her. No one ever gave her a name.

I imagine that little boy still sees her years later. Still reaching for him from around every corner.

9.

I left for school early the next day, sharing my sacred morning coffee with Dad instead of Cash. He seemed positively giddy that I'd asked him for a ride, and there was always something contagious about my dad's good moods. I teased him about his unshaven face, about his half-untucked shirt, his wild hair. And he played classic rock on full blast in the car, rolled the windows down as we entered the school parking lot, and belted out the chorus to "Carry On Wayward Son," earning him some cheers and laughter from the kids walking by.

"And you wonder why I don't ride with you." I grabbed my bag from the back seat, shaking my head at him.

"What!" Dad joked. "Everyone should listen to Kansas first thing in the morning. It really gets the blood flowing."

"Whatever you say, weirdo."

"Are you thoroughly embarrassed, though? Cause if not, I don't think I've fulfilled my dad duties. We can take another lap around the parking lot."

"Oh my god." I quickly threw open the passenger door and leapt out of the car, Dad cackling from the driver's seat.

I was pulling one strap of my backpack onto my shoulder when I saw Cash's truck pull into the lot. I was about to give in to the magnetic pull of him when the sound of my name broke the spell. I turned to find Porter jogging toward me. He looked like some kind rom-com teenage dream in a black moto jacket.

"Hey," Porter huffed as he slowed to a stop in front of me. He looked over to where my dad was locking up the car and gave him a nod. "Hey, Mr. Green."

"Ah, Mr. Dawes, gracing Wolf Ridge High with your presence before third period?" My dad smiled and started to walk toward the school. "I'd better see you in class this afternoon, kid."

Porter gave my dad a playful salute and then turned his attention back to me.

"So, I wanted to ask you if you were busy today after school."

I had no control over the sudden confusion and disbelief that splashed over my face.

"I'm...no?"

Porter laughed. "I just wanted to go scout a party location."

My face relaxed slowly back into a smile.

"Oh, right. Gotcha. Why do we need some special location, though?"

"Because if we're gonna do it like Gatsby, we gotta go big or go home, Green."

I was acutely aware of Cash watching us from his truck. I allowed myself the smallest glance in his direction, then fell into step beside Porter, heading toward the school entrance.

"All right. Wild Gatsby party location scouting. What kind of place did you have in mind?"

"There's a spot just outside of town I figured we could check out. Meet me by my car after last bell?"

He held the door for me and followed me inside. We were engulfed by the noise and commotion of slamming locker doors and morning conversations. Porter smiled at me as he started to back away. He raised his eyebrows, waiting for my response. I pressed my lips together, fighting off a smile.

"Yeah. Sure." I nodded once.

Porter nodded back, still smiling. He turned to head in the opposite direction, suddenly colliding with a body in his path. As he stumbled a bit, I saw Cash standing there, anger all over his face, eyes locked on Porter. The smile dissolved from Porter's face, and he reflected Cash's anger right back at him, the two looking like wolves circling each other, ready to go for the throat at any moment. That angry darkness looked out of place on Porter; on Cash, though, the darkness fit almost too well, settling into his features like a shadow.

"Got something to say?" Porter spat, an edge to his voice that made me bristle.

Cash hardly flinched, just adjusted his backpack and shoved

past Porter, knocking his shoulder roughly. He walked by me without looking, brushing past me like I was a ghost.

I turned to watch him walk away, and when I looked back again, Porter was already halfway down the hall, disappearing around a corner.

Cash avoided me all day. It both eased and exacerbated the ache that the previous afternoon had left in my gut—I wanted so badly not to want him, but it felt like losing a limb to go a day with a strange, unspoken tension keeping us apart. It didn't help that my sweater was still heavy with the scent of him. I unlocked my phone a hundred times to text him, to reach out, to fill the sudden space between us with something, anything. I only sent one: you never disagreed with me when i said you wouldn't need me once you left. He didn't answer.

By the end of the day, I'd convinced myself I didn't need to feel guilty. I'd written it, even—repeated it a hundred times in the margins of my notes. *I belong to no one. I belong to no one. I belong to no one.* Even while I carried the light purple outlines of his fingers on the backs of my thighs—*I belong to no one.*

Porter was leaning against his car when I walked out to the lot after the last bell. He had his back against the passenger side door, one ankle crossed over the other, one hand in the pocket of his jeans, that moto jacket unzipped to reveal the white tee underneath. The darkness I'd seen in him that morning had lifted from his face, which brightened even more when he saw me, sending my insides into a gymnastics routine.

Porter didn't drive an old hand-me-down car like most of

the kids in Wolf Ridge. His dad owned two car dealerships in the city, so they were one of the wealthiest families in town, and Porter drove whatever new car his dad leased for him every year. His current ride was a black hard-top Jeep. It was almost too perfect, like he'd picked it to go with his outfit.

"Ready?" He stepped back from the car and pulled open the passenger door, gesturing for me to get in.

I didn't know that I *was* ready. The whole thing felt like a scene out of a movie I was in but had never gotten the script for. Was everyone else in on the joke? *Was* it a joke?

I climbed into the passenger seat, and for some reason, it felt a bit like climbing into the seat of a roller coaster—excitement and anxiety and unease and contentment washed over me all at once. The inside of the Jeep smelled like aftershave, the pine tree air freshener hanging from the rearview mirror, and the bag of freshly laundered track clothes on the back seat. The screen in the dash lit up when Porter turned the ignition, the speakers blaring that poppy, overplayed Chainsmokers song the top forty station in the city couldn't stop playing. Porter must have noticed the face I made, because he quickly tapped a button on the console, and the radio switched over to Bluetooth, picking up music from Porter's phone, which he dropped into the cup holder between us. The car filled with the sounds of a familiar alt-rock band I had in my own music library, and I gave Porter an impressed nod.

"And here I thought *all* rich kids were uncultured swine," I teased him, buckling my seat belt.

Porter laughed, buckling his own and backing out. "Nah, just most of us."

I tried not to notice Cash walking to his truck as Porter drove out of the lot. He definitely noticed us, though. I let myself look over just long enough to see him lighting the cigarette between his lips as he watched me. Us. Porter Dawes and me. I looked away again, dug my fingernails into my palm, and mentally recited, *I belong to no one.*

Porter hung a left on Getty and headed toward the south side of town. He stopped at every crosswalk, even if no one was in it. I watched his hands in my peripheral vision, studied his fingers wrapped around the wheel. They looked strong and sturdy but soft. I kept trying *not* to notice them. I looked out my window instead, pleasantly surprised by the sun that was starting to show itself through the afternoon clouds.

"So, are you gonna tell me why you looked like a little kid whose balloon animal I popped when I asked you about you and Cash Peters yesterday?"

Porter's question caught me off guard. I looked over at him, hoping my face hadn't fallen into the usual defensive expression. I tried to force neutrality, to keep my jaw from clenching. But after witnessing their icy exchange that morning, it felt like discussing Cash was treading on dangerous ground.

"I didn't know I looked like that," I lied. "Why do you wanna know, anyway?"

Porter shrugged. "Just trying to make conversation. Poor attempt, I know. Just seemed sort of weird to start talking about the weather with a girl I've known since grade school."

"Yeah. I guess you're right. But it's not like we've been all that close. You don't exactly exist on the same plane as I do."

"What do you mean?"

I shrugged. "I mean, you're kind of in your own world, and I'm in mine."

He looked amused. I narrowed my eyes, unsure why his nonchalance and easygoingness were making me so irritated. Maybe I just wasn't used to people acting that way. I was used to spending my afternoons with Cash, sharing cigarettes and angst. Porter's willingness to be in a good mood felt unusual to me. Maybe, I thought, Porter was immune to Wolf Ridge's sickness.

"What?" I prodded, his smile making me anxious.

"Wolf Ridge doesn't really allow much space for too many different worlds, Wyatt. I hate to break it to you, but I think your bubble is self-imposed."

Porter looked from me to the road and back again while I sat there with my jaw a bit slack. Was he right? Had I created a bubble where Cash and I could wallow in peace? Did I incubate the town's sickness there like some kind of emotional petri dish?

"You look surprised." Porter took a right onto the Parkway, which ran parallel to a wide swath of abandoned farmland. Rolling hills spread way, way out into the distance until they ran into a sudden, dense tree line.

"I guess I never thought of it as self-imposed," I admitted.

"Maybe because Cash wanted you to think you didn't have a choice in the matter."

I didn't tense up at the mention of Cash's name this time. I didn't feel that same rush of defensiveness. I just looked over at Porter, at the farmland rolling past the driver's side window, and considered the possibility that he was right. I remembered how I'd started to fade into the scenery freshman year, becoming barely more than background noise to anyone but Cash. How I'd started to mold myself to fit only him, forgetting about everyone else I knew.

"Where are we going, anyway?" I changed the subject, folding my arms protectively over my chest. I didn't like talking about Cash behind his back. Even with the tension and weirdness between us, it didn't feel right to assume bad things about him, about his intentions with me.

"Just right up here." Porter accepted my shifting gears gracefully and didn't push it. I looked up ahead and saw a dirt turnoff approaching, marked by a sudden break in the old rotted fence. Porter turned down it, the Jeep bumping along. I kept my eyes ahead, searching for whatever secret spot he'd found for our party.

"So, you wanna have our party in the middle of an empty field?"

Porter laughed. "Hang on. It's right up here."

Sure enough, behind the slope of a hill, a building suddenly materialized. It was an old barn, but a big one, with a tall silo beside it and a wide open area of packed dirt around it. Porter parked the Jeep outside it and turned off the engine, gesturing toward the barn with one hand.

"This is it," he proclaimed. "C'mon, let's check it out."

We both got out of the car, and I pulled my sweater tighter around my body. Cash's scent was fading from the fabric, replaced by the smell of Porter's Jeep. I wet my lips and hesitantly approached the wide barn doors.

"How did you find this place?"

"Used to come out here and set off fireworks in the summer sometimes, me and some of the guys from the track team. I was trying to think of someplace sort of out of the way and off the radar, and I remembered this barn was here."

I looked up at it and nodded. "Let's go in."

Porter rolled one of the barn doors back, the wood creaking and groaning. The inside was dim and dusty, sunlight peeking through the slats in the walls. I stepped farther inside and turned in a slow circle, taking it all in. There was a rickety-looking ladder that led up to a loft, but otherwise, the barn was empty. Just the bones of what it probably used to be.

I nodded slowly, giving Porter my best smirk of approval.

"Nice digs, Dawes."

"We've got some generators at the house that I can bring out. Put up some lights, set up a sound system. We'll need to figure out a few filming angles. I figure we can put together a montage of the party and then end it with some kind of reenactment from another chapter so it has what Vaughn actually wants."

"You're taking this project *way* more seriously than I anticipated."

Porter grinned. "Well, when it went from school project to barn party, I got a little more invested."

"Something tells me you've got much bigger plans than I do."

Porter put his hands on his hips, surveying the interior of the barn. "Yeah, probably. Don't worry about it."

I laughed and shook my head. "I'll try not to."

I kept catching myself staring at him—almost as often as I caught him staring at me. My cheeks flushed with heat, my chest tightening in an unfamiliar, excited way. I tried to remember a time when I hadn't had to ask for attention, and I couldn't. But here was Porter, this boy I had always known and never known, grinning wildly at me, unable to look away.

I was wary, but starting to wonder if I had to be.

I realized I'd been smiling and staring for an uncomfortable amount of time. I looked away, cleared my throat, and pretended to be very, very interested in the ladder that led up to the loft.

"Ah, wait." Porter jogged back out the barn door and leaned into the Jeep, starting it. He turned the stereo all the way up, the barn filling with sound. He chose one of those poppy but somehow still haunting Taylor Swift songs that I only listened to in secret. And then there was Porter Dawes, dancing his way over to me, mouthing clumsily along with the lyrics.

The laugh I doubled over in was foreign, catching me as suddenly as a seizure and holding me just as long. Porter reached out and offered both hands to me, and I was still laughing when I took them. He pulled me to him, wound one arm around my waist, and swayed me gently along with the beat of the song, which echoed beautifully through the barn like that place, that strange ghost of a place, had chosen us rather than the other way around.

"Do you take all the girls to creepy abandoned barns and dance with them to Taylor Swift?" I asked, grinning up at him. "Is this how it goes?"

Porter stepped back from me, lifting my hand so I could twirl under his arm. I spun right back into his hold, another laugh spilling from me like it had been inside my chest with the lid twisted tightly shut until I'd loosened it. Or until Porter had.

"Of course. And it's a different creepy abandoned barn and a different Taylor Swift song every time. I keep it interesting."

We danced, and he twirled and dipped and held me until the song ended, and it felt easy and simple. The usual veil of Wolf Ridge's sickness must have lifted somewhere between the Parkway and the dirt road that led to the barn. Or maybe I'd just forgotten about it. Forgotten about the darkness that lived under all the floorboards in our town. Forgotten about the puddle of blood on the top step. It wasn't that Porter had suddenly taken up all the available space in my thoughts. It was just that he made it easier to put those other things away.

He seemed to build a sturdy dam where there was usually a free-flowing river.

It could have been seconds or minutes or even days that we spent with our faces inches apart, his arms still around me even after the music ended. I was the one to break the spell, pulling back from his hold, a nervous smile coming to my lips. Porter ran his fingers through his hair, looking just as surprised as I felt, just as flustered and taken aback. He didn't try to hide it, though. He just stood there with a content kind of confusion in his eyes, half smiling at me.

"What kind of lights do you think we should use?" I blurted out, turning away from him, my eyes sweeping over the ceiling of the barn. I just needed to look at anything but Porter Dawes and that dumbstruck expression on his dumb, pretty face.

Porter chuckled. He clearly wasn't interested in pretending. It was both refreshing and terrifying.

"Well, we want a twenties vibe, right? Lots of black and white and gold, sort of like a New Year's Eve party? My mom has these tiny twinkling lights she puts up at Christmas. We can hang a bunch of those from the ceiling."

I chewed on my bottom lip, trying to imagine it. I had never planned a party in my entire life.

I looked at Porter and lifted an eyebrow. "Gearing up for a position on the fraternity party planning committee, Dawes?"

Taking jabs at him was all I had to keep my head right. I was cuss words and cigarettes. Not someone's prom date.

"Hey, maybe. My skills are more vast and varied than you know, Wyatt Green."

I rolled my eyes, once again fighting a smile and losing.

"Yeah, whatever. So, we have a place, and we have some ideas for decorating. You wanna be in charge of invites? I'm sure you've got the whole county following you."

"Eh, more like the greater tri-county area. But yeah, I'll handle that."

He was grinning, and I shook my head, finding it difficult to believe that this goofy, flirtatious version of Porter Dawes was the real one. The version of Porter Dawes I had imagined was the one Cash had created for me—douchebag rich kid, only ever looking out for himself. It hurt a little, how many things I was discovering Cash was wrong about in just one day spent outside his immediate orbit.

The sun was already starting to disappear. I wrapped my arms around myself, bracing against the chill that was steadily thickening with the twilight outside.

"I think we've got ourselves a party, yeah?" I meandered over to the barn door, glancing back to give the inside one more look.

"Yeah, I think so. Few more pieces to put together, but at least we have a place."

Porter pulled the barn door shut behind us. He followed me to the passenger door of the Jeep, reaching for the handle to open it.

"What is this, nineteen fifty?" I grabbed the handle before

he could get to it, but that only started an impromptu wrestling match, both of us trying to open the door. There was that laughter again.

And on the drive to my house, Porter let me scroll through the music in his phone, and I made fun of him for the fact that he had Taylor Swift but not The Smiths, and he did his best impression of how I looked when we were in AP lit—surly, as he put it. And when he pulled up outside my house, I threw my arm out across his chest and demanded he not come around to open my door, because no matter what he thought, we were *not* in a music video for a country song. And I jogged across my front lawn, pulling my house key from the pocket of my backpack, and Porter beeped the horn to scare me, and I threw up my middle finger before I went in. And I leaned against the closed door once I was inside, and the entire world felt like it had been picked up and shaken out like a dirty rug, and everything felt a little newer and more awake.

My dad appeared in the foyer, looking at me through his black-framed glasses, a mug of coffee in his hand and this look on his face that was somewhere between confused and a teasing grin.

"Nice afternoon?" he asked.

I rolled my eyes, and Dad nodded.

"Good talk," he said, disappearing into the kitchen.

Last November

LOCAL WOMAN FOUND MURDERED IN HOME

Wolf Ridge—forty-two-year-old Lydia Green was found deceased in her home in Wolf Ridge on Tuesday. Green had multiple stab wounds, and the medical examiner determined that her death was a homicide. Investigators searched the immediate area and found no evidence of a murder weapon. Police say the home had not been forcibly entered. No arrests have been made, though police believe the suspect may be local to Wolf Ridge. Investigators are seeking any information regarding the case.

10.

My mother came into my room that night. She sat on the edge of my bed, pushed my hair back from my forehead, and whispered my name. I usually kept my eyes shut when she did this. I knew if I opened them, it would be to an empty, dark room. I knew if I looked, she'd disappear. So I closed my eyes tighter. Tried to keep my breathing even. Tried to keep her there. But she said my name again, and again, which she didn't usually do. She usually just sang to me as I tried to memorize the way the bed felt with the weight of her body on it.

"Wyatt." She said it again. "Wyatt, baby."

Her voice cut into me, deep stabs with a dull knife, so I opened my eyes, if only to make her go away, to make her stop saying my name. And there she was. The outline of her body was sleep-blurred but there. Even in the dark, I could see the spatter of freckles across her nose, the little smile on her lips as they formed my name again—"Wyatt. Baby."

"Mom?" I whispered. I was paralyzed by something—fear or grief or happiness—so I just watched her. She touched me, and I felt it, felt her there. I sat up a little, finally finding the will to move my limbs again. I studied her in the dark, trying to memorize her as best I could before she inevitably left again, before my room and house and world went back to being empty of her voice and touch. She didn't say anything for a while, just smiled at me in that soft, sweet way she used to. She always looked at me like I was still an infant, still delicate and innocent. Maybe to her, I always had been.

She reached for my hand, and when she took it, hers were freezing. Her touch was more urgent than before. She pulled on my hand, the smile fading from her mouth.

"Look at what he did to me, Wyatt."

She pressed my hand to her middle. My palm met the soaked red fabric of her shirt—and then something smooth and warm and unfamiliar. I felt my stomach lurch, my jaw go slack as I pulled my hand back and found it wet with blood. I scrambled farther away from her, grasping bedsheets and pillows and shoving my back against the headboard.

"No. No, Mom. Mom." I was pulling in desperate breaths, my lungs full of deep, heavy sobs. I closed my eyes to shut her out, willing her to go away, to leave me alone. I covered my ears to block out the sound of her calling my name, and I felt the warm blood on my palms touch the sides of my face. My hands erupted into violent tremors, a scream bubbling up in my throat as my mother's icy hands reached for me, her face desperate and scared.

"Look what he did to me, Wyatt. Look what he did to me."

I screamed and sobbed, holding my hands out in front of me, watching the blood drip from my palms.

The sudden light that poured into my bedroom from the hallway must have startled me awake. My mother was gone, my hands clean, the sheets no longer soaked in red. Dad's arms were around me, his voice an anchor.

"Hey, hey. Baby. It's okay. Wyatt, it's okay. It was a dream. You're all right."

I weakened in his hold, sobbing into his shoulder. My fingers curled tightly around handfuls of his T-shirt. And while he held me, I tried to get the sound of my mother's voice out of my head, but all it did was echo and echo and echo—*look what he did to me look what he did to me look what he did to me.*

The next time I woke up, I was on the couch, a blanket tucked around me. There was a note on the coffee table in Dad's handwriting: *Take it easy today.* I checked my phone. It was past one, the afternoon sunlight forcing its way through the slats in the blinds. I'd gone downstairs with Dad after the dream, and we'd both eventually fallen asleep on the couch, an old movie marathon playing on the TV. My phone screen was cluttered with notifications—texts from Quinn, mostly, asking where I was. One from Dad during his lunch period, checking in on me. I sighed and dropped my phone back onto the coffee table, pushing myself up and off the couch. I put on a pot of coffee, moving around the kitchen on autopilot, trying to settle into easy routines and keep my mind busy with things I could actually understand.

While the coffee brewed, I texted Quinn to tell her I was fine. I leaned one hip against the edge of the counter, my finger hovering over Cash's text thread. He'd been the last one to send something. It was time stamped right after I'd left the parking lot with Porter: what are you trying to do?

Dad's favorite mug was on the counter, so I filled it with coffee, then added a little spoonful of hot cocoa mix—Dad's and my favorite. I knew being home alone wasn't going to make the afternoon go by very easily. I could already hear the ghosts milling around, starting to scratch and whisper from inside the walls. I thudded my palm against the wall in the kitchen, trying to silence them.

My phone chimed from the counter. The screen lit up with a new text message.

too good for us uncultured swine today?

I'd almost forgotten that Porter and I had exchanged phone numbers the day before. I'd almost forgotten Porter entirely. It came back all at once, a memory I actually wanted to relive. Finally, a good reason for my stomach to do a backflip.

Pretty much, I wrote back. I carried my coffee to the garage door and unlocked it, nudging it open. It was cold out there, and I was grateful for the warm clothes I had on. Porter's text had reminded me that I had a party to plan, and I knew we had a pretty impressive collection of Christmas lights somewhere in the garage. My mom had loved Christmas, and I had loved watching my dad cuss and kick the ladder over while he hung the lights every year.

He hadn't hung them last year.

I took a sip of coffee and set my mug on Dad's workbench, surveying the stacks of boxes that lined the far wall of the garage. They were mostly labeled in Mom's messy handwriting. I spotted a box labeled X-MAS LIGHTS and pulled the stepladder over to climb up and get it down. My fingers grazed a small stack of paper on the top box. I wrapped my arms around the box and carefully brought it down to the garage floor. On top of it was a collection of newspaper clippings and low-quality black-and-white photos printed on computer paper. A headline on one clipping caught my attention first:

LOCAL WOMAN FOUND MURDERED IN HOME

The entire stack was newspaper clippings and printouts of online stories about my mom's murder. Most of them were new to me. I hadn't really followed the media's coverage of what had happened. My dad had shielded me from the press, chased reporters off the lawn and kept me out of school for the two weeks that followed Mom's death. I'd never considered that he might have been following the news stories, much less that he had been doing it in secret to protect me from it.

I went through the small stack—maybe even too small. There wasn't much interest in the death of one woman in some little nothing town in northern Vermont. Most of the stories were from local papers, and they all said basically the same thing: no suspects, no advances in Wolf Ridge murder case, state and local police baffled by lack of evidence. Those didn't rattle me. It was the photos that accompanied the articles that shot ice into my veins. Old photos of my mother, my own yearbook photo, even my parents' wedding photo, all printed between columns of text recounting how my mother was found by her teenage daughter in the upstairs hallway. No murder weapon. No fingerprints. No signs of forced entry.

I got through the articles and came to a handful of photos I hadn't seen before, my rib cage suddenly feeling too small for the air my lungs needed. They were crime scene photos. They had been taken after they'd removed her body, but that almost made them worse. The mess was unobscured by her form. Blood stretched from one side of the hallway carpet to the other. A desperate smeared handprint on the wall. Dad must have gotten copies of these pictures from the cops; he'd grieved by quietly doing his own investigating, like staring at these photos could manifest some kind of answer for him.

The investigators had concluded that my mom had been attacked in the bedroom and tried to drag herself down the hallway. My memory was mostly a blur of blood and screams and sirens. The photos, though, weren't faded or distorted by time. They hadn't been carefully dissected and compartmentalized by a fraught attempt at self-preservation. They were tangible. Seeing them sharpened the edges of my memory.

The last thing in the stack was a more recent article, dated only a few weeks ago. It had been printed from the internet, but I didn't recognize the name of the website it had been posted on. It was the bolded headline across the top of the page that shook me—

WHY ARE PEOPLE DYING EVERY NOVEMBER IN THIS SMALL VERMONT TOWN?

I skimmed the article below it. Some journalist from the Midwest had put together the pieces and found out about our November Sickness. Someone had cared enough to write about it, to point it out. The article was essentially a timeline of the previous fifteen years, at which point the writer had hit a brick wall in trying to obtain death records. I was too flustered to read it carefully. If the November Sickness was real, that meant it could keep infecting us. It meant that flicker of it that I'd seen in Cash, the flicker that was steadily growing into a five-alarm fire, could hurt him. Or me. Or someone else in Wolf Ridge.

I folded up the article and shoved it in my hoodie pocket, putting the rest of the stack back where I'd found it. I pulled down the box labeled X-MAS LIGHTS, hoping Dad wouldn't notice his stashed memorial had been disturbed. I wanted to run straight to Cash and show him what I'd found. I wanted to shove the article about the November Sickness into his hands and tell him I told him so, I knew it was real, I knew there had to be something bigger than us going on in Wolf Ridge. But when I set the box of lights down on the kitchen table and pulled my phone from my pocket to text him, it was Porter's name I saw on my screen.

Want some company?

I wet my lips, the folded paper in my hoodie pocket practically searing through the fabric. I was desperate to show it to someone—anyone, really. I wasn't sure it would feel real until I did.

I texted back: yeah, pick me up after school

Oh now you're making demands?

I rolled my eyes, if only to counter the smile.

don't then, I responded.

I'll do it if only to tell you face to face that you are not the boss of me.

I glanced at the clock on the microwave. School got out in twenty minutes. I was still in sweatpants and hadn't even brushed my teeth.

Fine, I wrote back before charging up the stairs. Outside my bedroom door, I stopped, took a deep breath to steady myself, and looked inside, thankful for the early-afternoon light. There was my bed, the blankets thrown back, pillows tossed aside. Dad had practically carried me out of there the night before—I'd been too hysterical even to put one foot in front of the other. But the room was empty. The ghosts were quiet. The sheets were clean, the same pale blue they always were. Still, I chewed my lip as I stepped inside.

And while I hurried to throw on some clothes and brush my teeth, I could feel my mother behind me, watching. I wished, then, that I had let her talk last night, let her tell me what she needed to say. I wished I hadn't been too afraid to ask her the question the cops seemed to have given up on finding the answer to: *Who did this to you?*

Three Novembers Ago

During freshman year, Joel Norman came to school with four guns in his car. A few handguns from his father's gun safe and a shotgun from his family's garage, the one he'd learned to hunt with.

He sat there in the school parking lot in a hand-me-down gray sedan. He was stoic, staring straight ahead, smoking a cigarette. We made eye contact, Joel and I, and I looked away quickly, his gaze heavy as lead.

When Joel shot himself in the parking lot after everyone went inside and we all heard the shot ring out from our homerooms, I wondered if that memory was real.

In Joel's car, the police found all the guns and hundreds of rounds. And on the passenger seat, a list of names. People he'd intended to use those guns on before he decided to start with himself instead.

My father's name was on the list.

11.

At the barn, I helped Porter unload the small generators he had heisted from his family's shed and all the boxes of lights we'd collected from our garages. He shut the back of the Jeep, picking up the last box and carrying it inside. "So, we just need some backup gas containers for the generators, but these two with full tanks should last us the whole party."

"What about music?" I asked, kneeling down to open a box, making a face at the tangled mess of lights inside.

"Oh, yeah, that's under control. Dean's got a whole system he's gonna bring—speakers, all that." Dean was on the track team, another guy at Wolf Ridge whom I had known but not known since we were kids.

I got to work untangling lights while Porter moved the generators to the back corner of the barn. He came and opened another box, pulling out neatly rolled coils of tiny LED lights.

"Your mom is much better at putting Christmas lights away than my dad is," I laughed, holding up the mess of tangled cords I was trying to sort out.

"She's a little anal-retentive about that kind of stuff. Standard mom behavior, I guess."

At the mention of mothers, I could sense the lightness in his voice harden a little. His smile visibly dimmed. I studied him a moment, pulling a tangle out of the cord I was working on.

"You can say the word *mom* around me, Porter," I said gently.

"Yeah, I just—I didn't want to make you—"

I shook my head. "Let's just get it out there. My mom's dead. It's okay. I'm okay. It's not a secret." I put on my best reassuring smile. "Seriously. It's okay. I won't break."

"I never really got the feeling you were all that breakable," he said, and I was suddenly—almost painfully—aware that it mattered to me what he thought. It was an unfamiliar feeling, one that rushed to my cheeks in a flash of heat despite the barn being so cold.

I cleared my throat and stood, looking up at the rafters. I could feel Porter watching the side of my face.

"How are we going to hang these?" I asked him, propping my fists on my hips.

He shrugged. "I'll climb up there and walk across the beams."

"Are you high?" I let out a laugh. "You'll fall and break your neck."

Porter widened his eyes. "No, seriously? Will I? It's always been a dream of mine."

"Whatever, break your neck, then. I'll make sure they play Taylor Swift on a loop at your memorial."

"Ah, the only true way to preserve my memory." He put a hand over his heart and laughed. "I'll be fine. You just bring strings of lights up the ladder and hand them to me."

I tried to hold back the gasps that kept escaping me as Porter climbed up the ladder and stepped off the edge of the loft and onto one of the thin rafters. He tested his weight first, and then, when the beam was sturdier than either of us expected it to be, he started to carefully make his way across. He draped the lights in long loops, letting them hang low. I imagined them looking like a starry night sky when we turned them on.

I stood on the loft with the untangled light strings, connecting them and handing them off when he needed another.

"Hey, can I ask you something?" I handed Porter the next string.

"Sure. I'm kind of a captive audience right now."

I'd been debating since Porter had shown up at my house whether I wanted to tell him what I'd found. So much of me felt like I knew him, like I could trust him—but there was still a part of me that was clearheaded and remembered that we had only really started talking two days ago. Still, he'd grown up in Wolf Ridge, just like I had. He'd been here for all those bloody Novembers.

"Do you think Wolf Ridge is..." I tried to find the right

words, ones that wouldn't make me sound insane. "You've noticed what happens around here in November, right?"

Porter was bent over, looping a string of lights around the rafter. He stopped for a second and looked over at me.

"I dunno. I guess. I mean, it's kind of hard not to."

I nodded, watching him make his way back for more lights. When he got to me, he stopped for a second, making it a point to catch my gaze.

"Why do you ask?" He took the lights from my hands and started working on the next rafter.

I thought of the article I'd found, now tucked under my schoolbooks on top of my dresser. I chewed the inside of my lip, grappling with whether or not I wanted to say anything else.

"I dunno." I shrugged. "Just been hard for me not to notice, too."

We were both quiet as he draped the lights over the last rafter and carefully returned to the loft. He stood there, looking at me, and the way his eyes softened felt like a physical weight against my chest.

"Let's plug these in and check out how it looks, yeah?"

He smiled and touched my elbow as he stepped past me to get to the ladder.

We both climbed down, and Porter jogged across the barn to the extension cord he'd hung from the rafters, plugging it into one of the power strips he'd connected to the generators he'd left just outside the barn's back door. The lights came on, turning the rafters into a twinkling night sky. A smile split my lips. I folded my arms and turned in a slow circle, looking up.

"Okay, I'll give this one to you. It's pretty great." I shoved my hands in my back pockets and dropped my eyes back down to Porter. He was grinning, and he shrugged.

"What can I say? I had a vision."

"Yeah. Like I said: gunning to be the president of the frat party planning committee."

"Hmm, something tells me you wouldn't be interested in that first lady position."

I lifted my eyebrows, more amused than I wanted to admit.

"Yeah, no, I doubt you'll catch me anywhere near a frat party."

"Okay, so maybe you won't be rushing Kappa Kappa whatever, but you *are* going, right? To college?"

I involuntarily flashed back to being in the bed of Cash's truck, when we'd talked about college, about what I wanted to do after high school. After Wolf Ridge. But it was still nearly impossible for me to see what *could* come after Wolf Ridge. It was all I had ever known, and even with its violence and crowded cemetery, it was home. I was comfortable in its darkness.

All I could do was shrug, leaning my shoulder against one of the barn's support beams.

"I guess. I mean, it's sort of the logical next step. But I'll probably just take classes at the city college."

Porter unplugged the lights and switched off the generator.

When he turned back to face me again, I was surprised to see what looked like concern beginning to deepen the lines in his forehead.

"The city college?" he asked, furrowing his brow even more. "I thought you were one of the top students in our class."

It was the first time I'd ever felt ashamed of my grade point average. He made it sound like I'd won some grand prize and had chosen to take the consolation prize instead.

"Yeah. Well." I pushed off the beam and stood up straight, holding my elbows, feeling protective of the pang of disappointment in the center of my rib cage. "I just don't think I can see myself anywhere else."

"Why?" Porter probed, despite my body's cues that I wasn't all that interested in talking about it. "What's keeping you here?"

I stared at him for a long moment. Long enough for the tension of the silence to get to us. He knew the answer to his own question, I was sure of it. After all, I walked around with it blinking above my head like a neon sign: *broken girl broken girl broken girl!* Again, I was aware of the reality that still existed outside of the barn, this safe place we had found.

This would normally be the point where Cash would collapse in on himself. When he'd light up a cigarette, watch it burn just to look at something other than me. But Porter never looked away. Instead, I did. I turned my entire body away from him and walked slowly toward the open barn door.

"Wyatt," he called after me. I expected him to let me walk

away, to let me slam my internal doors in his face. Cash always let me go. So when I heard Porter's feet smacking against the ground as he jogged after me, it startled me, and my breath caught when Porter's fingers wound around my wrist and gently pulled me back.

"Look, I'm sorry. I know you feel like we don't know each other, and this is probably me overstepping, but I just think you can do better than this place. I think you can do better than what this place has done to you." He stepped around in front of me. "I think you can do better than what Cash Peters has made you believe about yourself."

I looked down at his hand, fingers still loosely gripping my wrist. I may have been Broken Girl, but I wasn't weak. I wasn't one of the girls who turned into a crumbling sandcastle at the mere mention of Porter Dawes. I was barbed wire compared to them. I was cigarettes and cuss words. Being vulnerable had never worked out for me much before, leaving me more than apprehensive about letting it happen again. Especially with Porter Dawes, the boy I knew but didn't know.

"What's with you and Cash, anyway?" I was surprised by the sharp edge of my words. I pulled back on my own reins and softened my tone. "What happened?"

Porter let go of me and let out a sigh, pushing his fingers through his hair. I watched the bones in his wrist flex, followed the curve of his hand down to where his arm disappeared into the sleeve of that black moto jacket.

"I told you," he said, his shoulders lifting and dropping in a quick shrug. "He thinks I did something I didn't do, and he's had it out for me ever since."

"What does he think you did?" As much as I wanted to understand the tense, silent anger that stood like a brick wall between them, I also wanted to feel sorry for myself, yet again faced with the realization that I didn't know Cash as well as I'd imagined.

"It doesn't matter, because it isn't true. To be honest, I think he just needs a target. He needs someone to dump all of his pent-up shit on."

The normal protective urge I had when it came to Cash began to creep down into my fingertips, threatening to curl my hands into fists. But I shook the feeling out, shoving my hands into the back pockets of my jeans instead. For once, I didn't want to cling to the story of Cash I had built inside my head. For once, I wanted to hear someone else's version.

"What does he think you did?"

I could tell Porter was struggling to decide whether or not to tell me. He shifted his weight, paced a few steps, chewed his bottom lip. All at once, I wasn't sure I really wanted to know anymore.

"It's okay. You don't have to—"

"No, I actually think you should know. I thought you already did. Cash has never really liked me, so I always assumed that was why you quit acknowledging me—because Cash had convinced you I was a piece of shit," Porter said, interrupting me before I could shift the gears of our conversation back to safety.

"Cash has never told me anything about you. All I know is that he's never exactly been your biggest fan." I paused long enough to swallow back some of the shame that was tightening around my throat before I added, "I never had a reason for not speaking to you."

"You did, though. You told me the other day. You thought we existed on different planes, right? And I told you that you and Cash were the ones who chose to stay separate from everyone else once we got to high school. Or he chose it, and you went along with it."

Porter's voice wasn't accusatory or sharp. Instead, it felt like an adult trying to explain something sad to a child, careful not to let it hurt too much.

"Okay. You're right. Maybe I did go along with it. But I'm here now. I'm making an effort. So tell me why Cash didn't want me to." I pulled my hands from my pockets, holding my elbows again, as if preparing for whatever blow he was about to land.

Porter watched me for another moment, studying me, like he was still on the fence about telling me. He stepped over to lean his back against the passenger side of his Jeep, then pulled in a deep breath.

"Last summer, I was dating Kristen Daniels," he began, and I remembered: homecoming queen dream, with honey-brown hair that brushed her elbows and legs that went on and on. But just as quickly as I remembered her pretty face, I remembered the smashed barrier at the top of Lawson's Bluff. The spiderwebbed windshield of her dad's truck. The groups of girls holding each other and sobbing in the school hallways for weeks, decorating her locker with cards and flowers that eventually turned brown and littered the scuffed floors with dead petals. I remembered sitting beside her in world history, how she always flashed me a smile even if I rarely offered her one back.

I nodded, and Porter went on.

"There was this party at one of the track guys' houses. He graduated last year, threw the party to celebrate heading off to college in California and getting out of Vermont. Cash was there. Shit, everyone was there. But I remember being surprised to see him, especially without you. He came with one of the other guys who worked at the diner with him last summer. Anyway, I was there with Kristen, but we were doing our own things, you know? She was with her friends, I was playing drinking games with some of the guys. She was on the other side of the living room, and then when I looked for her again, she wasn't there. I just assumed she'd wandered off. People were out in the backyard, too—there was a pool, and it was summer, so a lot of people were swimming. I didn't think much of it."

I nodded again, letting him know I was listening. I was trying to remember the party and why Cash had gone without telling me, without trying to drag me along. That summer, I had taken a trip with my parents down to Cape Cod, so I figured it must have happened while I was away. Still, I could see Porter tensing, hesitating more and more as he spoke, choosing his words slowly and carefully, like he was trying to make sure he told the story the right way. I fed off of his anxiety, my heart pumping a bit harder.

"So," Porter went on, "a while goes by, and I don't see her. I'm upstairs with a few people, passing around a bowl in one of the bedrooms. And after a bit, I go looking for her to see if she wants to leave. It was pretty late, maybe two or three in the morning. She wasn't downstairs, wasn't outside. So I told her friends to give her a lift home, and then I left."

Porter shrugged, wetting his lips. I waited, knowing that couldn't be the end of the story.

"A few days later, those pictures came out," he said through a heavy sigh.

It only took a second for the memory to come back, in pieces at first, and then clearly—returning home from Cape Cod to hear about the naked pictures of Kristen Daniels that someone had posted on Snapchat under a fake name, then shared with nearly the entire student body of Wolf Ridge High. By the time the photos were reported and taken down, they had already been downloaded and shared, sent through texts and private messages, and she had been publicly mocked and shamed. I remembered how when school started weeks later, someone had stuck the printed photos on Kristen's locker. And only weeks after that, she'd driven her truck off Lawson's Bluff. Kristen was the first casualty of last November, soon buried under the loss of my mother. Under nightmares and hallucinations of blood-soaked carpet. The record player and the crackling melody it sang on repeat.

While I sorted out the timeline, we stood in silence. But even once I thought I had it all down, something was still missing.

"So, what does any of that have to do with Cash?" I asked, grasping at the loose ends.

"After Kristen..." Porter paused, searching for words. "After she passed away, I ran into Cash in the bathroom at school. He shoved me, started going off about how he knew it was me, that I'd been the one who took the pictures and posted them. He said he saw me leaving alone that night. He told me she'd killed herself because of me, that it should have been me who went off that cliff."

It was almost too much to take in. I felt like I was too small for what Porter was trying to fill me with. My seams were pulled tight, the image of Kristen's truck careening off the bluff playing on a loop—the barrier smashed to splinters; her white knuckles on the wheel; strands of that honey hair stuck to the tears on her cheeks; the sharp crack of branches and rocks colliding with metal and glass. The piece of the story I couldn't understand was Cash's anger. He had barely ever acknowledged Kristen's existence. We'd left her funeral early, sat up on the bluff and smoked instead, watched the yellow police tape on the broken barrier dance around in the wind.

But less than a week later, I'd found my mother dead in the upstairs hallway, and everything else became static.

"But...you didn't. You wouldn't." I shook my head, feeling like I was trying to solve a math problem. "Right?"

"Of course I didn't do it. She broke up with me a few weeks after that, and I guess Cash thought it was because she thought I'd done it, too, but she didn't. I think she knew who did."

"If she knew, why didn't she tell someone?"

Porter shrugged, sighing. "I have no idea. Best guess is that she was humiliated and assumed turning the person in would just lead to more bullshit she would have to deal with. I just wish she had told someone she was... I wish someone had known how she felt."

After he spoke, we stood in silence for a few long, quiet moments. The sun was setting behind the barn, the temperature dropping steadily, and I hugged my sweater tighter around myself. Porter sniffled, the cold beginning to turn the tip of his nose pink. I watched him, pulling the threads of his story into a needlepoint image in my head, trying to make out what it became. It was just a constellation of bad timing and misunderstandings and broken tree bones. I felt as though I had to make a decision based on what I now knew—to believe Cash or to believe Porter—but he wasn't asking me to decide anything. He was just standing there in a halo of sadness I didn't recognize on him. Whoever had posted those photos of Kristen was trying to hurt her. And being hurtful didn't fit what I knew of Porter.

But Cash was definitely capable of placing blame where it wasn't deserved. Spite and anger fit him like a tailored suit.

"It's getting cold." I pulled my sleeves down over my hands. "Maybe we can come back tomorrow and finish setting up."

Porter brightened.

"Yeah, of course. Come on, I'll take you home."

That time, I let him open the passenger door for me. And as he drove, I studied his profile through sideways glances, noticed the smooth curves of his fingers around the steering wheel. In the glow of the dashboard lights, I made my diagnosis and decided Porter was probably immune to the November Sickness. It wasn't the decision I'd thought I would make, but it felt like the first good one I'd made in a long time.

Two Novembers Ago

BODY DISCOVERED NEAR GIHON PARK

Wolf Ridge—The body of a man was found in a vehicle near Gihon Park on Thursday. The man was identified as Ben Foster, thirty-three, of Burlington. The medical examiner determined that Foster died of a brain aneurysm. Foster's family is urging police to investigate further, citing the victim's young age and good health.

"There is no way my son died of natural causes all alone in his car, hours from home," Foster's mother, Diane, stated on Friday morning. "Something happened to him, and the police aren't doing anything about it."

A memorial service for Foster will be held next Saturday in Burlington.

12.

The newspaper article I'd pocketed from the garage was laid out on my bed. The edges of the printer paper were already curled from how many times I'd read the short piece. My eyes kept going back to the block type of the headline:

WHY ARE PEOPLE DYING EVERY NOVEMBER IN THIS SMALL VERMONT TOWN?

It felt like a direct question to me, and it was frustrating not to have an answer.

I pressed the printed pages flat against my calculus textbook. I had skimmed the paragraphs a hundred times, as if I might find some secret code I hadn't noticed before. Some message sent directly to me, some voice shouting an answer in the spaces between the words.

Jennifer Scolitz—that was the journalist's name—had mapped out the history of the blood and darkness that overtook Wolf Ridge every fall, going back fifteen years. I ran my finger along the creases in the paper, following a trail of car wrecks, suicides, murders, house fires, and freak accidents that led up to my mother's death, where the article ended. Perhaps it was her story that had sparked this woman's interest in our dark cloud of a town. I scanned the paragraphs again, revisiting some of those raincloud memories. I wondered what it was about my mother's murder that had caught her attention all the way in Illinois, what had made her open up her laptop and start diving into the black water of our history.

The article had been printed from Jennifer Scolitz's personal website, which told me she worked for the *Winthrop Daily Times,* a tiny, small-circulation newspaper from an equally tiny town on the border of Illinois and Wisconsin. I spent the better part of an hour looking at photos and reading articles from that newspaper—write-ups of Memorial Day parades and Easter breakfasts and memos on bike safety. There were pictures of the shore of Lake Michigan, of little kids at the opening of new playgrounds and rec fields. The broken parts of me wanted to know Winthrop's secret, to know what bloody thing had happened there that had since been hidden by smiling kids and sunny lakeshores. I wanted to know what the town had tied cinder blocks to, pushed out into the harbor, and sunk to the bottom of the lake. But more than that, I wanted to know who Jennifer Scolitz was and why she had written a pages-long exploration of Wolf Ridge's bloody rap sheet.

I went back to Jennifer's website. I skimmed over her blog posts again, scrolling to the bottom as if I might find something new. And there, at the very bottom, I did—a small contact link. When I clicked it, it opened a new email addressed to jscolitz@winthroptimes.com.

My fingers hovered over the keys for a few long moments. How was I supposed to start? Was there even a way to *ease in* to telling her who I was?

Hi, Jennifer.

I chewed my bottom lip. Curled my fingers into anxious fists and relaxed them again.

My name is Wyatt Green. Lydia Green was my

I stopped. Tapped the backspace key.

I'm Lydia Green's daughter. I would really like to talk to you about what you wrote.

I included my cell phone number and hit send. The email window disappeared from my screen, revealing the photos of Winthrop underneath. Kids in a model sailboat contest. A young-looking woman mayor presenting a key to the city to a little boy in a wheelchair.

I opened up a new browser window and typed in wolf ridge vt.

The first photo to appear was of my mother. She was leaning into my dad's shoulder, but the rest of him was cropped out. The link read: Home invasion ends in brutal murder. I kept scrolling, eventually finding a more recent piece about a new suspect in the case. I remembered the last time the sheriff had come by with news about that suspect, an out-of-towner he thought had tried to rob us. I scrolled through the article until I found the man's mug shot—hollow eyes, dark hair, and the sharp, angular face of someone strung out. Norman Lewis. I'd researched him thoroughly, including finding his high school yearbook photo on the school's website. He'd been cleared quickly—he was in a holding cell in Adams County the night of the murder—but still landed in prison on assault and drug charges.

I'd never believed it was him, just like I didn't believe it was whatever new suspect the sheriff had. I refused to believe someone from outside Wolf Ridge had randomly decided to kill my mother in November.

I shut my laptop and let the silence in my bedroom wrap itself around me, settled into it, let it anchor me back down. The house felt like it had been tipped on its side, trapped under the weight of all that not knowing. It was a feeling I kept hoping would go away with time, but the house never righted itself. I was stuck in the almost, in the in-between. My fingertips burned like I'd barely brushed the edge of an answer, only to have it evaporate. To disappear into the walls like all the ghosts in the house did. To taunt me softly from under the floorboards, with whispers of things I couldn't understand drifting down from the attic.

I wondered if there were ghosts in Winthrop. I wondered if anywhere was really safe from all that darkness. I wondered if Jennifer had black water inside her mind, threatening to pull her under at any moment.

I pressed the home button on my phone, lighting up the screen. It was 3:17 a.m. The house was quiet, aside from the soft hum of the television coming from my dad's room. He always fell asleep with it on. I wondered if the noise and light helped the bedroom feel less like a tomb. Before my phone screen went dark, a text came through, the vibration startling me.

Cash.

are you awake?

I pressed my lips together, fingertips hovering over the screen, poised to respond quickly like always, like my limbs were trained to come when called. It had been a few days since we had spoken, a feat I'd never managed in the years since I had decided to sew my heartstrings to him like a piece of shoddy patchwork pinned to a fine tapestry.

your light is on. come outside.

Goose bumps prickled over my arms, and I felt my heartbeat pick up speed. I hadn't planned to ignore him forever, but this was too sudden—I hadn't practiced what I would say, hadn't even convinced myself why I was shutting him out to begin with.

My body decided for me, and I found myself downstairs, pulling my jacket on and shoving my sock feet into my boots. I unlocked the front door and opened it, careful not to make too much noise. Cash was standing a few feet away from my front steps, hands in the pockets of his black jeans. It was too late for him to have just gotten off a shift. He rarely worked past midnight.

"What are you doing, Cash?" My voice came out laced with more exhaustion than I intended.

"I came here to ask you the same thing, Wyatt," he answered calmly.

I wrapped my arms around myself, gripping my elbows tightly, already beginning to shiver a bit in the cold. While he waited for me to speak, he raised both eyebrows, expectant.

"I just needed a little time," I blurted out through a sigh.

"Time? Why? Time to hang out with Porter Dawes?"

My body stiffened involuntarily. "Time to sort out what I'm feeling."

Cash took his hands from his pockets and pushed his hair back. It was one of the things he did when he was trying not to get irritated, a frustrated tick I knew too well.

"Is this because I said I wanted to leave?" he asked. "Because you've known all along I had no plans to stay here. And it always seemed like you were supportive of that."

"Supportive?" I shot back at him. "So silence equals support?"

Cash threw his hands up. "You never said you were going to

stay here. I guess I always assumed you would be leaving, too. I'm having a hard time figuring out why you'd want to stay."

I remembered Porter saying almost the same thing to me earlier that afternoon. No one could understand why I wanted to stay in Wolf Ridge, why I *had* to, even. I couldn't leave my dad alone with the ghosts. I couldn't leave him alone in that house with his picture shrine and the boxes of my mother's things.

"This isn't just about you wanting to leave, Cash. And I think you know that."

I stared at him, clenching my teeth hard enough to make my jaw ache. His expression softened, his hands coming to rest at his sides.

"You know we can't."

His words were thick with pity. They stung like a lungful of pool water.

"We can't what, Cash? I think you mean *you* can't. Because I'm perfectly capable of not treating you like a toy to tide me over until I find something better."

There she was—the girl I thought I'd begun to lose sight of. Barbed wire and razor blades. Her reappearance caught Cash off guard. He pushed his fingers through his hair again, giving it a frustrated tug.

"Do you really think that?" he choked out, his face suddenly desperate. "Is that how I make you feel?"

The pain in his voice was like a knife in the center of my chest. On the rare occasion that Cash let himself be vulnerable in front of me, I melted into an unrecognizable version of myself.

It took me a moment to collect the pieces of my voice in my throat. I breathed in deep and slow.

"Once you leave Wolf Ridge," I began softly, "I'm not going to matter."

He opened his mouth to speak, but I lifted my hand to stop him before he could.

"It's okay, Cash. I figured it out a long time ago, and I'm fine with it. I think you should leave this place—I know you should. But if I'm going to be the last one left here, I have to start letting go of this." I gestured between our bodies. The space became tangible, something I could grip and use for support, use as some kind of reassurance that it was, in fact, possible for me to stand on my own.

"So, letting go of this means cutting me out of your life entirely?" His voice broke, the shards of it cutting into me. A sob caught in my throat without warning, my jaw going slack and my eyes stinging. I fought it tooth and nail, trying to sharpen my own edges, not wanting to become the wilted flower he was capable of turning me into.

But then one petal fell. And then another. I stood on my front step, a forgotten orchid, an unsalvageable watercolor painting after a flood. He forgot me. He flooded me. He was every disaster I had ever lived through.

The frozen front lawn crunched under Cash's feet as he bridged the gap between our bodies. He took my face in his cold hands, caught my trembling lips with his own. Muscle memory made my fingers curl tightly into his jacket, my mouth desperate against his. I fought the instinct, flattening my palms against his chest and pushing hard, turning my face away from his.

"No. Cash. Stop it."

Cash pulled my face back toward his, tangling his fingers into a fistful of my hair, keeping me close, shoving his lips against mine again. My arguments fell on deaf ears. Cash's body was firm and unmoving against my steadily weakening hands. His lips dropped to my neck, and I cried into his shoulder.

We were on a cliff's edge that was beginning to crumble under our feet.

We were always and never.

Forgotten orchids. Ruined watercolors. His colors melted into mine.

"Come with me." He breathed the words into the centimeters between our mouths. I let him take my hand, let him pull me to his truck, left my bed empty and my father asleep with the noise from the television.

There was an urgency in Cash that I didn't recognize. I was hardly aware of where he was taking me, just hyperfocused on him—the muscles tensing in his jaw, his white-knuckled grip on the steering wheel. By the time he pulled hard on the parking brake in his own driveway, I was far away, deep in the losing battle I was having inside my head. I always let him win. I always handed over the broken pieces of myself like pitiful offerings.

His dad's car was missing from the driveway. The windows

of the house were all dark. I followed him to the door, practically jogging to keep up as he pulled me along, his grip tight on
my wrist. My legs felt heavy, like I was waist deep in dark water.

We spilled in his front door, both of us breathless for no
reason. He kicked the door shut behind us, fingers turning the
bolt in one quick motion before they slid around the back of
my neck again, pulling my face to his. The thick silence of the
house made our breathing sound louder. I could hear our lungs
filling up with the desperate breaths we took.

Cash shoved my jacket off my shoulders and onto the floor,
shaking his off right after. My pulse was picking up speed, the
thudding in my throat making my ears ring as Cash's hands
made their way down my torso.

"Where's your dad?" I panted, my hands suddenly erupting
in shakes, fingers trembling against Cash's sides.

"Out of town," Cash practically snapped at me, pressing
his lips to mine. He dropped his hands to the backs of my
thighs, and out of habit, I wound my arms tightly around his
neck and pulled myself up into his hold, wrapping my legs
around his waist and crossing my ankles against the small of
his back.

Our bodies were as obedient as the tides.

We were reduced to skin and bone and need.

But as Cash carried me blindly through the house, stopping
to hold me against the wall just outside his bedroom door, my
mind began to drift away from me again, going somewhere
else while he dragged his lips over my collarbone.

I closed my eyes and found myself in the passenger seat of Kristen Daniels's truck.

I watched her grip the steering wheel, heard her let out a sob, felt the truck lurch forward as she slammed her foot down on the gas pedal. I forced my eyes open, like trying to wake up from a bad dream. I dropped my hands to Cash's chest and pushed, arching my back away from the wall he had me pinned to.

"Cash. Stop."

Cash pressed his body harder against mine, wrapping his fingers around my wrists and gripping them tightly.

"Shh," he whispered against my lips.

I turned my face away. I was beginning to panic—why was I suddenly so afraid to let him have me? What was it about the hunger and urgency in his movements that overwhelmed my body with tremors?

I wilted against the wall.

"Please," I whispered. The girl that had sliced at him on my front steps must have stayed there and let me leave without her. There, pinned between Cash and the wall, I was the sad little girl the ghosts in my house usually reduced me to, all nightmares and tears.

Cash let go of my wrists and took my face between his hands. I felt his fingers brush away tears I'd hardly noticed. I closed my eyes again, my legs dropping from around Cash's hips until my toes touched back down on the floor.

This time, when I shut my eyes, I saw Cash. He was

somewhere I didn't recognize, somewhere outside of Wolf Ridge, somewhere with tall buildings and busy streets. He was holding the hand of a girl whose face I couldn't see, but I could see his, and he was happy. Without me. Far away. Gone.

"We can't. I don't want to. You have to let me let go of you," I pleaded with him, now just a heap of sad, sorry bones against the wall. He held me up, drew his hands down the length of my arms until he could lace his fingers with mine.

"Why would I want you to let go of me?" he answered, leaning his forehead down against mine. "You're the only one who will ever love me like this."

Like a shitty game of word association, Cash's words drew up another memory—Porter, standing outside of the barn. *I think you can do better than what Cash Peters has made you believe about yourself.*

I shook my head, the weakness Cash drew out in me starting to turn into anger, like a fire beginning to burn its way through my insides.

I flattened my palms against his chest and pushed again, this time putting some space between our bodies. Having even that tiny bit of power over him threw gasoline on the flames. I shoved him again. Hard. He stumbled back a step. Even in the dark, I saw his face shift from disbelief to anger. The shadows that outlined his features seemed to darken.

"You get off on it, don't you?" I snapped at him, flames leaping off my tongue. "Me needing you. Me loving you, and you not giving a shit."

I saw his eyes narrow, as if he was trying to read my face like a book.

"This is about Dawes, isn't it?" he answered. I tried to convince myself the darkness in his eyes wasn't making me nervous.

"Oh, get over that, will you? This is about you and the bullshit you've been feeding me for years to keep me around."

His breathy, amused chuckle was too familiar. So was the lift of his eyebrows. The way he looked at me through his eyelashes.

"Is that what you think?" he asked, hair falling into his eyes.

I nodded. "I think you're so afraid to be alone that you'd say just about anything to keep me around."

Cash wet his lips slowly with a look that sent a wave of goose bumps prickling over my arms. He let my words settle around us like dust. I watched him. Pressed my back against the wall, trying to put more space between us.

It was like I could see the sickness waking up in him again. That dark violence he kept inside was loose from the cage it slept in.

When he lifted a hand to draw his fingers along my cheek, I couldn't stop myself from flinching.

He noticed.

"Looks like you're the one who's afraid, Wyatt."

In the second it took me to lift my hand to smack his away, he had my wrist, his fingers tightening around it until I gasped in pain, his knuckles going white.

The flames in me went from candlewick to wildfire.

My will to fight him wasn't as strong as the deep, almost painful need I had for him. So when he yanked my body back against his, I pressed into him, but the glare didn't leave my eyes.

He ducked down suddenly and hoisted me up over his shoulder, hardly giving me a second to object. I pulled at his shirt, writhing as he carried me through the doorway into his pitch-dark bedroom. Before I could even growl any of the anger burning my tongue, my back hit his mattress, and I collapsed into the unmade sheets. I breathed in deep, practically melting into the scent of him. Cedarwood. Bergamot oil. It weakened my defenses long enough for him to hook his fingers into the waistband of my sweatpants and panties and start pulling them down, but I grabbed his wrist and pushed him away, my heart beating in my ears. The fire raging in me erupted from my mouth when I screamed, fighting against him and pushing at his chest, the flames stoked by fear and anger.

It was like the sickness had stolen Cash away and what was left, this dark animal, was out for blood.

My blood.

I needed the stronger version of me. My fire was going to die down. In its place, the cold sting of fear had already started to ice over my rib cage.

"Get off of me, Cash."

The softness of my voice gave me away. It fed him. He gripped my wrists hard enough that I gasped, my fingers scratching desperately at his arm. I watched him come undone on top of me, his face splashed with a kind of anguish I barely recognized on him.

Every nerve ending in me was firing at once, sending me into another fit of tremors that I knew weren't from excitement. I closed my eyes, trying to go somewhere else again, somewhere like the bed of his truck in a month that wasn't November, when he touched me like I was glass, when he was gentle and forgiving of the way I always weakened under him like my bones had left my body.

"You think everyone in this town is sick, Wyatt?" he said, voice edged with pain. "*You're* sick. This is the way people are. There isn't anything wrong with our town—people are just shitty. It's not my fault you don't want more, that you don't want something better, that you want to be stuck here. It's not my fault I'll disappear and you'll be trapped forever."

He loosened his grip on my wrists just enough for me to free one hand and smack him hard across the face. Then my hands found the center of his chest, and I shoved him, using all the strength I had right then to try and free myself from under him.

Cash may never have felt for me the way I felt for him, but he had never intentionally spat fire at me. He had never hurt me on purpose. My body had never been a matchstick he'd been so focused on striking.

"You're mine," he breathed.

He wedged his knee between my thighs, trying to pry them apart. His hold on my body tightened, and I felt myself forgetting to struggle. Outside, it had started raining. And I closed my eyes and tried to remember what it had felt like that afternoon in his backyard, kissing his smiling lips while it poured around us. My eyes burned with tears, and I crumbled into sobs under him.

I felt his body halt. Felt his grip on me falter. I closed my eyes and kept crying, prepared for him to take what wasn't being offered, some part of me broken enough that I questioned if I had ever given him a reason to believe he didn't own all of me.

The sudden absence of his weight on top of me made my eyes snap open. He'd climbed off of me and was standing at the end of his bed, pulling at his hair, face painted with a kind of desperation I'd never seen him wear. He looked like he'd scared even himself, and he stared at me with wide eyes as he took a few steps back.

"Fuck. Wyatt. I..."

He turned suddenly, snatching up his keys from the dresser as he hurried out of the bedroom, and I heard the front door open and slam shut again.

The sharp tension that had built up in my limbs released, and I sobbed harder, curling into a tight knot on Cash's unmade bed, realizing he'd only left because he would have hurt me more if he had stayed. I tried to find my own edges again, tried to remember the shape of my own body, repeating the same words out loud as I tried to keep myself from disappearing—

I belong to no one I belong to no one I belong to

13.

A gray sunrise filled the sky like the aftermath of a forest fire. The light snow that was falling may as well have been ashes, peppering my hair but disappearing when it hit the pavement. By the time I had walked the few blocks to my own street, the flurries had stopped, leaving me damp and shivering.

I felt outside of myself.

I was separate from my body, watching from across the street as the girl with wrinkled clothes and unbrushed hair walked forward like an apparition, a ghost caught in the loop of a tragedy. That girl couldn't have been me. Where was her barbed wire? Her sharp edges? That girl was edgeless. She was hardly distinguishable from the air around her.

When I reached my front door, I half expected to find another crime scene. This November was gearing up to be just as bad as the last one, so what would another body be but a drop in the bucket? I searched my jacket pockets for my key, already imagining my father's shredded body on the floor of the foyer, as normal as a piece of furniture.

My pockets were empty, but when I tried the knob, I found the door unlocked. The foyer was empty. The air in the house felt thin, that eerie early-morning silence taking up all the space. I shut the front door behind me and leaned back against it.

Before I could even let out the breath I'd hardly realized I'd been holding, my dad came bounding into the foyer from the living room in a rush of quick steps and a loud sigh of relief.

"Wyatt Julianna Green, what the hell were you thinking?"

He had his phone in one hand, and he pushed the other hand through his wild hair, eyes wide behind his black-framed glasses. He looked frantic, and I felt a pang of guilt so deep it seemed to go straight through me, nailing me to the door.

"I wake up and your bed's empty, your phone's just sitting there, the front door's unlocked, and you are nowhere to be found. I mean, are you fucking kidding me?"

I flinched when he swore, not out of shock but because of the pained, desperate way his voice sounded. I could tell he was trying to hang on to anger, but it was quickly dissolving into fear. And just as quickly, my bones were dissolving into dust. I let my chin drop toward my chest, my knees giving out like rotted wood. Before I was all the way to the floor, I was in my father's arms. He hooked one arm under my useless legs and wrapped the other around my hollowed-out torso, but instead of carrying me to bed like a child, like he always did when I broke, we settled on the floor together, a messy heap of what was left of us.

I heard his phone clatter to the ground next to us. I was tucked into his body, aching for the safety that existed only inside of his hold. Over his shoulder, my mother's photograph shrine watched us fall apart.

Dad smoothed my hair back but said nothing. I wanted to cry, wanted to show him I still felt something—anything— but I was emptied out. I forced my burning eyes to stay open, because every time I closed them, I saw the black of Cash's eyes, the vacant space where the person I knew used to be. November had taken him from me. And somehow, the hungry, violent thing it left behind had managed to take me from myself, too.

"I'm sorry," I finally said, my cheek against my dad's shoulder.

He nodded a little and touched a kiss to my forehead. The stubble on his chin scratched lightly against my skin, and the familiar, gentle feeling of it was like permission for me to settle down.

"I'd tear the world apart before I let anything happen to you." Dad's hold around me tightened a bit. "So for the sake of the rest of the world, you've gotta help me out. Let me know when you're going somewhere. And Wyatt?"

I lifted my head to look at him. He studied me for a second, pushing my hair back from my forehead.

"Remember what Mom used to tell you."

Even before he finished his sentence, Mom's voice was already in my head, like a radio playing in another room: *Wyatt, don't be the tide. Be the moon.* I knew that was what Dad was talking about. Mom used to say it all the time, used to write it on the whiteboard on the fridge and on the napkins in my lunch bag. I still wasn't entirely sure I knew what it meant or how I was supposed to live by it. If anything, I felt more like the tide than I ever had—constantly shifting, never able to figure out just where or what or who I wanted to be.

But I nodded anyway. I was just glad he hadn't asked where I'd been. The idea of him finding out, of having to tell him about the darkness November had left in place of Cash was enough to unsettle my empty stomach.

Once we were both to our feet and Dad had given me a tight, warm hug, he backed toward the doorway to the kitchen.

"I'll get coffee on."

He gave me the best smile I figured he could muster, and I headed up the stairs. I needed to shower off the night. It was sticking to my skin, heavy and uncomfortable.

In the bathroom, I turned the lock and faced the mirror, frowning at my own reflection. The circles under my eyes were purple and dark with exhaustion. My cheeks even looked hollow, like I'd been deflated. The rest of my face was colorless and blank, framed by a mess of dark hair, tangled and tied in a half-hearted twist against the back of my neck.

Slowly, I unzipped my jacket.

Lifted my shirt off in slow motion.

My wrists were ornamented with black-and-blue fingerprints.

The same dark watercolor marks were peeking out from under the top of the sweatpants I pushed gingerly down my hips, watching the bruises appear like a shocking piece of art concealed behind a curtain. I stood there naked in front of the mirror, trying to identify the stranger staring back at me. She was Cash's Wyatt—obedient, needy, pitiful. While the November Sickness made some of us hungry to hurt others, it made a few of us hungry to hurt ourselves. This girl, this version of Wyatt Green, was the latter.

I turned the shower on.

Inched the temperature as high as it would go.

And while I stood under the stinging hot water, I felt that Wyatt burn away.

I rode to school with Dad, and even though we'd both brought coffee from home, he still stopped at our favorite gas station for hazelnut dark roast and chocolate frosted dough-nuts. I almost wanted to laugh at how fucked up our broken little family was—normal teenagers who disappeared from home in the middle of the night on a weekday usually ended up grounded, but I ended up with breakfast sweets and Dad letting me pick the music in the car.

I was halfway down the hall to Mr. Vaughn's class when Quinn suddenly appeared in front of me, cutting me off. I peered at her over the rim of my coffee cup.

"So, you skip school, then ignore all my texts? The fuck, Wyatt?"

I could tell she was trying to keep her tone light, but it was laced with genuine irritation. Another blow of guilt straight to the center of my chest.

"Hey, I'm sorry, okay?" I hooked one arm around her neck and walked alongside her down the hall. "I was dealing with some stuff. But I'm good now."

Quinn looked sideways at me, eyes narrowed warily. If I could have looked at myself right then, I probably would have worn the same expression. I didn't even believe myself, but I was determined to let it be a self-fulfilling prophecy. If I believed I was fine, maybe I would be.

"Whatever you say," Quinn said through a sigh, her gaze dropping to her phone. "Wait, hold up a second. Developing story." She stopped us both short in the middle of the hallway outside Mr. Vaughn's room. "You didn't tell me you were throwing a party."

"What?"

Quinn held her phone up, a Facebook invite on the screen.

"Ain't No Party Like a Gatsby Party? Hosted by Porter Dawes and Wyatt Green?" she read, scrolling down. "Holy shit, there are like a hundred people on this invite list."

"Oh my god," I groaned, pressing my palm to my forehead. "I knew he was going to go overboard with this."

"With what? How long has this been a thing you haven't told me?" Quinn demanded, landing a playful punch on my arm.

"Ow! Like, a few days! I hoped he wouldn't make a big deal over it. It's just for the video project." I glanced inside the open classroom door; Porter's seat was still empty. "What are you and James doing for it?"

"Definitely not anything as fun or awesome as throwing a Gatsby party." She frowned at the invite again, scanning the info on the page. "Much less a Gatsby party in some mysterious barn outside town." She grinned as she looked over at me. "How much time have you been spending all alone with Porter Dawes in some abandoned barn, Wyatt Green?"

"Oh my god, Quinn—"

"We actually live there now." A voice from behind us made Quinn and I both whip around to find Porter walking over. "Going for that minimalist vibe. Living off the grid. Reconnecting with nature. This is actually a housewarming party cleverly disguised as a school assignment."

Even as a smile wrestled its way onto my lips at the sight of him, I was suddenly very aware of the bruises under my clothes, the waking nightmare of the black in Cash's eyes that I was playing on perpetual repeat in my mind. All at once, I felt ashamed of the girl he'd stolen the night before. There were still shreds of her trapped under my skin. I still felt responsible for how helpless she had rendered herself, more so once I was caught in Porter's gaze, like stage fright under a spotlight. Like he knew. Like he had seen that girl walking home that morning, tangled hair peppered with snow.

"Well, you can count on me being at this thing." Quinn

shut off her phone screen, and the grin she was wearing made my cheeks flush.

I widened my eyes at her, pressing my lips together.

"I'll see you guys inside," she added as she backed into the classroom, shooting finger guns at me, sending my palm to my forehead.

"God, she's..." I shook my head. "Quinn."

Porter stepped around in front of me and leaned his shoulder against the lockers outside the classroom door, that swath of hair tumbling over his forehead. He was so strangely familiar, enough to loosen the tightness that grief and disappointment had wrapped around my limbs. I knew him, didn't I? He was the same kid from sixth grade I accidentally gave a black eye with a poorly aimed dodgeball toss. He was the rich kid everyone loved, who brought goody bags for the whole class every year on his birthday—September fifteenth. How did I remember that?

And still, a refrain kept playing in my head: *You don't really know him.*

"Don't you think you're going a little nuts with this party thing?" I lifted an eyebrow at him. "I mean, a hundred people? Are you *hoping* to get caught and have it shut down?"

"Wyatt. It's not like Gatsby was known for his quiet, tame dinner parties where people discussed politics and played Scrabble."

"You know he is a fictional character, right?"

Porter feigned shock, stepping back. "Wait, *what*? Gatsby isn't *real*?"

I rolled my eyes, stepping around him to the classroom door. Every one of my nerves seemed to fire at once when I felt his arm wind around my shoulders.

"Don't panic. We aren't going to get busted. It's not like we have neighbors to worry about." He gave me a playful pat on the back as he released me. "Don't be so scared that you might actually have a good time, Wyatt Green."

He winked at me before he dropped into his seat, and I couldn't figure out if the sudden heat in my chest was because I found it sweet or because I found it horribly embarrassing.

I realized, though, as I walked to my seat and set down my backpack, that Porter had been able to distract me from watching for Cash in the hallway. No matter how silly or annoying Porter was, rolling my eyes at him was significantly more enjoyable than thinking about the sad, broken girl I had washed down the shower drain that morning.

No matter how much I tried to feign normalcy and let one simple day go by without thinking of my mother's case, it rarely worked. Despite spending most of the day discussing party plans with Porter between classes, I still found myself leaning into my locker between fourth and fifth periods, scrolling on my phone, once again searching all the names of prior suspects. Typing those names into the search bar was almost muscle memory by then. Each time, I expected something new to come up, but nothing ever did. I searched my mother's name; I searched wolf ridge vt; I searched my own name and my dad's. Every search yielded the same results as always, the same articles and stories I'd combed a thousand times already. The same photos of my mother, the same headlines, the same brick wall.

While I scrolled, an email notification popped up, and I quickly opened it to see a message from jscolitz@winthroptimes.com.

Wyatt, glad to hear from you. Let's talk. Can you video chat?
    JS.

14.

I sat on one of the speakers Porter had set up in the barn, watching as he climbed the ladder up to the loft. He had a bag slung over one shoulder that had four GoPro cameras inside. I was still convinced Porter was going way overboard with the party, but instead of arguing with him, I just worked on making a playlist.

"Do you really think a school project is worth all of this effort?" I scrolled through his extensive Taylor Swift collection. "I mean, for a video? And how are we going to tie this in with a specific scene in the book, anyway? We can't exactly just film a party and convince Vaughn that it has anything to do with—"

"Quiet, young grasshopper," Porter interrupted.

I looked up from his phone to watch him attach a camera to one of the ceiling beams.

"I have a plan," he went on, offering me nothing else.

I waited a beat, lifting both eyebrows at him.

"Do you intend to clue me in on this plan at all?" I prodded, standing up and moving to the middle of the barn, folding my arms over my chest.

Porter glanced over at me, a grin splitting his lips before he turned his attention back to what he was doing.

"What, don't you trust me?"

I opened my mouth to answer him but realized I didn't have an answer. Even if he was being playful, the question knocked me off balance, the marks that Cash's sharp edges had left behind still raw and fresh under my clothes.

I wet my lips and collected my composure up off the floor, where it seemed to have fallen rather ungracefully.

"Whatever," I said, throwing my hands up. "But if I flunk this stupid project, I will personally tell Mr. Vaughn that you sabotaged me, and I will make sure the entire school—sorry, the entire *tri-county area*—knows the amount of space occupied by Taylor Swift songs on your phone."

Porter hopped down from the last step of the ladder, brushing his hands off, his grin brightening as he turned to me.

"Oh, I don't doubt it." He winked at me as he moved past, looking for another good camera angle.

Despite everything that had happened less than twelve hours before, I was exceptionally at ease. Whatever weight had been piled on my shoulders, I'd left it somewhere on the Parkway as we drove to the barn after school. I felt like I should build my guard back up, though—things had a bad habit of going severely south whenever I let it weaken too much. This was still Porter Dawes, after all. I still knew only a few pieces of him, no matter how good and safe and warm those pieces seemed: the dimple in his left cheek, his extensive and impressive collection of silly dance moves and The National albums, the way he said my name—so familiar, like it'd been his own name in a past life. In fifth grade, he was the only boy in our class to bring a valentine for Kelly Wilson, who'd been bullied viciously by the popular girls all school year.

But still, these were only pieces.

I shoved my hands into the pockets of my sweater to warm them, my fingers wrapping around the folded pieces of paper I found inside. The article. The reminder that I was still a resident of a town that imploded in on itself every November. I pulled the folded paper from my pocket, turning it over a few times in my cold fingers.

"Porter?"

He had climbed up onto one of the speakers and was reaching to attach a camera high up in the corner of the barn. When I said his name, he looked over his shoulder at me, arms stretched over his head. He noticed the paper in my hands, and when I didn't say anything else, he finished attaching the camera and jumped down, walking over to me.

"What's that?" he asked, offering his hand to me, palm up. I placed the article in it, pulling my bottom lip between my teeth as I watched him unfold the paper.

"My dad had it with a bunch of stuff about my mom. I found it when I was looking for Christmas lights."

I watched his eyes scan the paper, expecting him to shut me down, to tell me to stop believing in bullshit urban legends about Wolf Ridge, to stop trying to find something to blame for all the awful things that happened in our town. Porter looked at me when he was finished reading, what seemed like concern starting to deepen the lines in his forehead.

"Okay," he said, carefully refolding the paper. "What do you think of this?"

I had been expecting a different response so much that I was caught off guard by his question.

"I think…" I started, finding it difficult to grab hold of my suddenly racing thoughts. "I think there's something more going on here than people will admit. I have no idea what it is, but I feel like this"—I pointed to the paper—"is proof that I'm not the only one who sees it. Who knows it's happening. Someone was curious enough about it to write this article. So if this person sees it, why does everyone who lives here treat it like some kind of urban legend?"

While I spoke, Porter kept his eyes on me, listening so intently that I hardly knew what to do with his attention. I was almost overwhelmed by it, by the chance he was giving me to finally argue my case to someone who gave enough of a shit to listen.

"People here notice, Wyatt," Porter said. "They just prefer to look the other way. To pretend it isn't real. I mean, who wants to face that, you know? To consider that there's some kind of...I don't know. Some kind of evil here. It's almost too ridiculous to be a coincidence, you know?"

I nodded, blindsided by the fact that someone believed me. But I remembered the day Ms. Linney was arrested when we were in eighth grade, how Porter had sat two seats over from me, stone-faced and pale. How he'd stood stoically at Kristen's funeral, somehow looking like a lost little boy and a heartbroken teenager all at once.

I took the paper back from him and shoved it into my pocket, worrying my bottom lip between my teeth again. I could feel it starting to simmer deep inside my chest—the rush of every single thing I had ever wanted to say about our town, about my mother, about all the blood and broken glass we had been raised on.

"I've always felt insane for thinking it. That there's a sickness here. Like, something in the fucking water," I started as I began to pace around the barn. "It sounds insane, right? It does. But how the hell else can anyone explain it? Is it just in everyone's DNA here? It's a small town in goddamn Vermont, for Christ's sake. Who would pick this place at random to come kill some woman for no good fucking reason?"

Before anything else could tumble out of my mouth, Porter caught me by the shoulders, his hands inching down to grip my arms gently, keeping me in place.

"Hey." He dropped his chin, tilting his head to catch my gaze, which was still flying wildly around the barn, quick like my pulse. I locked onto him. I let him anchor me back down.

"Whoever hurt your mom, whether they were from here or not, was sick. And there wasn't anything you could have done to change that. You can't change other people. You can't fix them. And frankly, it isn't your job to. But you *can* change yourself. You can decide to look at this flaming garbage can of a situation in a way that...that will let you move on from it. Because at this point, that's the best thing you can do for yourself. Be selfish. Take care of Wyatt. She deserves it."

It was my turn to listen. And I did. I listened with every cell in me. Maybe I only knew pieces of Porter, but this piece, the one he was sharing with me right then, was one I thought I could trust. It was one that might be enough to convince me that maybe not everyone in Wolf Ridge had gasoline inside of them, waiting for a spark. And maybe it was the broken, messed-up parts of me that told me to do it, or the slow burn of the bruises under my clothes, but when I suddenly reached up and pulled Porter down by the back of his neck and kissed him, it felt like *that* was the best thing I could do for myself.

Porter didn't pull away. He didn't pry my fingers from his skin. He didn't sigh or whisper to me about deserving better than him. He didn't try to convince me not to feel anything.

He kissed me back.

I felt his hands fall to my waist, felt his fingers move gently toward the small of my back, let him inch my body closer to his as he parted his lips against mine. I felt the ice start to melt away from my bones. The razor blades under my skin dulled.

I moved my arms around Porter's neck and eased up onto my toes, letting his body press flush against mine.

He was, all at once, every good memory I had. He was writing himself into my history, showing up in the background of the photos of me as a child, the ones that lined the hallways of my house like old Christmas ornaments. This boy I thought was mostly a stranger showed me that I knew him better than I'd ever let myself believe. I could be a normal girl kissing a boy who wasn't just waiting for something better.

The kiss ended gently, in a careful separation of lips and blending of breaths, still only centimeters between us. When I opened my eyes, I was half surprised to find him actually standing there, to see it wasn't all some cruel joke or daydream. I eased back down off my toes, heat rushing to my cheeks as what I'd just done slammed into me, stinging me with something between embarrassment and excitement. Had I really just kissed Porter Dawes? Had he seriously just kissed me back? What planet was I on?

"Well," Porter began, loosening his grip on me, "that isn't exactly where I was expecting that conversation to go."

He must have noticed the sudden loss of color from my face, because he quickly shook his head and smiled, lifting one hand to the back of my neck.

"But don't get me wrong, I'm glad this is where it went."

I felt an apology bubbling up in my throat out of sheer habit and forced myself to swallow it back. Without it, I found myself speechless. Did I really have no instinct other than to recoil and apologize after showing someone affection? I was starting to see more and more just how fucked up I'd let myself become. I couldn't land on which feeling I wanted to feel the most just then and settled for confusion, letting out frustrated breath.

"It could be worse," Porter said, as if on cue. "A Taylor Swift song could have been playing."

"You know, now I'm kinda bummed one wasn't," I answered, letting Porter anchor me down again.

He grinned, then touched his lips to my forehead before he released me.

And that was it. Like nothing had happened. Like what *had* happened was totally normal and totally did *not* warrant me overthinking it and spiraling, as was my tendency. So I followed his lead and let it be.

"We can see how the angles look from here," he told me, showing me his phone screen. He'd opened an app that was streaming footage from the cameras he'd put up. The small boxes showed us standing there in the center of the barn from all different sides.

"Well, that's not creepy and over the top at all, Dawes," I chided him, laughing.

"You say creepy and over the top, I say the best project in the entire class."

It felt like a full-time job to keep my pulse steady while we stood there. It was taking way too much effort to stop myself from doing something embarrassing, like crying or telling

Porter that he was the only boy I'd ever kissed besides Cash. It was like I was determined to sabotage myself.

"Chapter three," I proclaimed. I propped my fists on my hips and surveyed the barn. "That's the chapter you're re-creating."

Porter grinned and put his phone in the back pocket of his jeans.

"You know chapter numbers off the top of your head? What are you, a walking encyclopedia of American literature trivia?"

I shrugged. "Let me guess—you'll be Gatsby."

"I mean, unless you want to be. I'm cool with a little twenty-first-century gender bending."

"Oh my god, no, you can be Gatsby. I think we're going far enough off the rails with this as it is."

Porter grabbed his backpack, pulling the zipper closed and tossing one strap over his shoulder.

"You haven't asked who I've cast you as."

I fell into step beside him as we walked out of the barn, pushing the heavy door shut behind us. "Something tells me it isn't Jordan Baker. Or Nick."

Porter opened the back door of his Jeep and tossed his backpack inside. I stood beside the passenger door, waiting for his answer, and somehow, I still felt like I'd left my broken body and slipped into a shiny new one. It felt clean. It felt stronger. But it didn't quite feel like mine yet.

"You know, I think people misunderstand the story. People swoon over Daisy and Gatsby like they have this great

American love story, but it's more a tragedy than a romance. Same with Romeo and Juliet. They teach us that the only way to love someone is to lose them. But I kind of think that's bullshit. Want to know what the real love story is in Gatsby?"

I felt myself smiling while I listened to him. I nodded, urging him to continue.

"Gatsby and Nick. Hear me out, I'm not even kidding." Porter was laughing, but he went on. "Nick is the only one who really gives a shit about Gatsby, who likes him for more than his money, who looks past all the shiny shit and sees that he's just a guy. Just some dude who loves a girl he'll never have. And who's there when Gatsby dies? Who's there at his funeral? Daisy? No. Nick is. There is more to loving someone than just being miserable over them. There are better options."

As Porter went on, it wasn't Gatsby and Daisy who played out the scenes in my head. It was Cash and me. Cash was my Daisy—the unavailable love, the one dangling his affections in front of me, keeping me around when the rest of the world forgot about him and he needed someone to fill the empty space. And maybe Daisy didn't tear Gatsby to physical shreds the way Cash had done to me, but she did it in her own way by abandoning him, by forgetting him, by choosing what was easy over what was right. Cash would choose a one-way ticket out of Wolf Ridge over me any chance he got.

"Would that make you Nick in this scenario, then?" I asked, studying Porter in the changing light as evening settled in, the sun sinking behind the barn.

He smiled in a knowing sort of way, opening the passenger door for me.

"No idea what you mean," he joked, still smiling at me as I sighed and climbed into the car, letting him close the door behind me.

While Porter walked around to the driver's side, my phone vibrated in my pocket. I pulled it out to see a text from Cash. His name on my screen felt like a swift punch to the gut.

please wyatt. i didnt mean to.

I shoved my phone back into my pocket, trying to fight off the lead building in my chest. Porter buckled his seat belt and flashed me a smile. I wanted to stay *here*, in the warmth of his passenger seat. But I could feel myself getting pulled back into the murky depths of Cash's hold on me, his grip only ever loosening and never fully releasing me.

At home, I hurried upstairs, checking the clock on the night table as I slid into my desk chair. It was 5:28, two minutes before I was supposed to video chat with Jennifer Scolitz. I sat down at my desk and opened my laptop, logging on, blinking at the image of myself that suddenly popped up on screen. That girl looked tired, looked aged, looked like she'd seen seventeen a few too many times. I tied my hair back with the elastic around my wrist, trying to make myself look the slightest bit less exhausted, but it only made me look suddenly younger, a little girl with dark circles under her eyes.

I wasn't sure what was making me so anxious. What was making my blood run a few degrees colder, my fingertips going icy. From behind the walls, I heard my ghosts. Tapping on the drywall, whispering into the vents. I put my earbuds in to drown them out just in time for an incoming video call from jscolitz to appear on my screen. I took a slow breath and clicked accept.

The image of me minimized to make room for a young-looking woman with dark curls and a pair of thick-rimmed glasses. Her brown skin looked clear and soft, the angles of her face going gentle when she saw me, a hint of a smile pulling at her lips. The kind of smile that said *I'm sorry for you* before she'd even spoken.

"Hi, Wyatt," she started, voice soft but affirming. "I'm really glad you reached out."

There was something inherently awkward about speaking face-to-face with someone I wasn't actually face-to-face with, the artificial closeness creating even more distance.

"I found what you wrote about Wolf Ridge," I said, keeping my voice low, aware that I wasn't alone in the house. "About the sickness."

Before I'd even finished saying the word, I wished I hadn't. The way her face contorted into confusion—no, concern—made my chest tighten sharply. I swallowed back the thickness the word had brought to my throat.

"The sickness?" she probed. I saw her pick up a pen.

"I mean..." I searched for words that wouldn't make me sound crazier than I probably already did. "There has to be some explanation, right? Something that makes sense of what's been going on here?"

Jennifer pushed her glasses up into her hair. Propped her chin on her hand.

"That's what I was hoping to find. That explanation. I'm not sure what I found, though. There was a lot of evidence of something weird going on, but not really anything that could explain it." She shrugged and sat up again.

The disappointment that settled over me must have shown on my face. She pulled her glasses back down and shuffled papers in front of her.

"I managed to get death records for the last fifteen years. But further back than that, I couldn't. And when I reached out to your sheriff, he shut me down at every turn. And look, that could totally just be small-town cop mentality, not wanting some out-of-state journalist poking around and stirring shit up baselessly. Or..." She trailed off, lifting her hands and sitting back in her desk chair. "Or maybe something's going on that they don't want people knowing about."

"There has to be," I said, with more urgency than I meant to. "Nothing about it makes sense, and I live here. I've watched it happen. I've seen what it looks like up close."

The corners of Jennifer's lips turned down. She set her elbows on her desk and leaned forward again, and I watched her chew her bottom lip in thought for a moment.

"Listen, Wyatt."

I braced for the quick letdown, for hearing yet another person tell me I was overthinking things, making it all up in my head. Jennifer opened her mouth to say something, then closed it again. She took off her glasses and studied me through the screen.

"When I was working in Detroit on a homicide beat, it felt like this...endless barrage of terrible news, and all I wanted was to find answers, to be able to point to something tangible and say, *this*, this is what's making people act this way. Eventually, all I could do was quit that job and move away and bury myself in pieces about the high school football team. The bake sale at the Rotary. I moved to a place where the worst news is cloudy weather, most days. And I moved here so that I could...*pretend* things aren't that dark. That people aren't always just black holes. That there's still good in the world."

I looked at the photo of Cash and me on my desk beside my laptop. His bright grin, something I could only trace back to that exact moment, something I don't think I ever saw again after that. I tried to fit the word *good* around Cash. Around Wolf Ridge. But their edges stuck out, cut into it, broke it into pieces.

"Why did you look into Wolf Ridge in the first place?" I asked, my eyes still on the photo. "Was it my mom?"

"I read something about your mom, yeah. It was in a police blotter I still tracked. For something so big to happen in a town no one had ever heard of and for there to be no leads, no real information...I got curious. And when I looked up your town and all I found were obituaries, I couldn't help but wonder."

I nodded.

"Wyatt," she started again, "what made you reach out? I

know you said you found what I wrote, but…it seems like something else made you send that email."

I pulled my bottom lip between my teeth, bit down until it hurt. Tugged my sweater tighter around my body, felt the lingering aches on my skin, the bruises I knew hid under the fabric, leftovers from when Cash gathered up the love I had for him and lit it on fire. I thought of his eyes, dark and empty, as he'd watched me reduce to ash under him. So lost, so far from that boy in the photo.

"I guess…I guess I just want to know why," I heard myself say. "I want to know why it happened, why it keeps happening. But maybe it was going to happen whether there was a reason to or not. Whether there was some cosmic shift or if it was just…badness."

She looked unconvinced. She studied me for so long I wondered if the video had frozen, until she finally nodded and took her glasses off, setting them aside.

"I wish I had more information. I wish anyone did. But I hit a brick wall. I don't think anyone knows what happened to your mom. And if they do, they aren't talking. So…I can't say if you're right or wrong."

But I'd stopped hearing her after *what happened to your mom*. I was out of my body, pinned against the ceiling, floating on the sudden, strange, inexplicable relief of *I don't think anyone knows*. For all the aching I'd done, for all the needing, wanting, craving an answer, I felt surprisingly at home in the idea that maybe there *wasn't* one.

"What else do you know about the deaths in your town?"

The curious tone she suddenly had brought me back down into my chair, watching her brow furrow through the screen. She jotted something down.

I thought of all the bad news, the ever-growing body count, the funerals, the suicide prevention assemblies at school. I thought of Ms. Linney's kids facedown in their bathwater. Kristen's truck tangled in the trees below the bluff. Cash's mom and her bathtub tomb. And my own mother in her quiet corner of the cemetery.

I looked at Jennifer, at her pen, poised and ready to write down whatever I said. And like I had with Porter, I suddenly felt listened to, believed, less like I was losing my mind. Like I was the only one seeing all the ghosts that crowded our town.

I felt miles away for a moment. All those obituaries and funeral wreaths dissolved under the soft rush of river water. Chattering teeth. Melting into a strange, still blackness I couldn't name but knew was inside of me.

From somewhere inside the walls, one of the ghosts whispered in Cash's voice.

Help me. I want to hurt someone.

"Too much," I finally said. "I know too much."

15.

I probably should have been more surprised to see the cop car parked in front of my house. I was walking home from doing homework at Quinn's the next afternoon, and there it was. But the sight of it barely made my pulse jump. In the year since Mom had died, I'd become so used to seeing cop cars in my driveway that never brought any answers that I didn't even give it a second glance before I let myself in the front door. I could hear voices coming from the living room, and after I'd dropped my backpack, I heard my dad call for me.

Sheriff Grant was sitting on the couch across from Dad, and they both stood up as I entered. The sheriff was wearing the same expression he'd worn the night my mom was killed—pained, but like he was making an incredible effort to keep it from showing. Finally, my body began to react. My blood pressure picked up. The back of my neck prickled with sweat under the light scarf I was still wearing. My dad and the sheriff both looked like doctors about to deliver bad news to family members in a hospital waiting room.

"What's going on?" I asked, wiping my palms on my jeans.

"Wyatt, Sheriff Grant came over to give us some news." My dad had his hands half inside the pockets of his black jeans, a nervous, awkward stance he assumed when he didn't want to say something. I remembered him standing that way in my bedroom door when he had first tried to ask me without asking me if I was having sex with Cash, if I was being safe. I cringed, both at the memory of that conversation and in anticipation of whatever conversation was about to happen.

"We've got a new suspect in your mom's case," Sheriff Grant said, as if my dad's nervousness was palpable enough that he felt it, too. "We needed probable cause to pick him up for questioning, but now that we have it, I wanted you and your dad to be the first to know."

As he spoke, though, I was spiraling away, leaving my body, tumbling back into the passenger seat of Cash's truck on the night he'd told me what he'd overheard at the police station. A new suspect. Maybe they knew who'd done it. When I closed my eyes for a second, trying to anchor myself in my body again, I saw the blood-soaked hallway carpet, the snow blowing through the open front door, fanned out over the floor in the foyer. That sickeningly haunting song playing on repeat.

"Wy? You okay?"

My dad's voice tethered me. I opened my eyes.

"Who?" I asked.

My dad took his hands from his pockets, taking a step toward me. "Wyatt—"

"He's not local," Sheriff Grant interrupted. "We're working with the sheriff's office in Addison County on this one."

"Wait, he's not from Wolf Ridge?" I asked, unable to filter the exasperation out of my voice. "That doesn't make any fucking sense." I shook my head.

Sheriff Grant's frown deepened noticeably, and my dad took another step toward me, maybe sensing my impending breakdown like animals can sense a storm brewing. The way I leaned against the wall must have been the last bit of approaching thunder Dad needed to know I was on the verge.

"Thanks for coming by to let us know, Sheriff," he cut in, stepping around the coffee table to guide Sheriff Grant toward the front door. "Really appreciate it. Keep us posted."

I heard them exchange awkward and hurried goodbyes before the front door shut and my dad was back in front of me, hands gripping my shoulders.

"This is good news, Wyatt," he said, leaning down to try and catch my eyes. "Maybe we'll finally find out what happened. Get some closure. Move on."

But I was shaking my head, moving out of his grip so I could pace freely around the living room. I felt like everyone around me was suddenly speaking another language, like I was the only one in the dark.

"I don't need the sheriff to tell me what happened, Dad. I know what happened. Someone from Wolf Ridge murdered my mother. I know it was someone from here. They have the wrong person."

"Baby, what are you talking about?"

"I know you know, Dad. I know you know about the sickness."

Dad let his jaw go slack before he pressed his lips together, pushing his fingers through his wild hair.

"You know just as well as I do that someone from Wolf Ridge killed Mom. Why are the cops looking in another county? Why is everyone in this town so dead set on ignoring the shit that goes on here? I know I'm not the only one who has noticed the body count this goddamn place has."

"Wyatt," Dad began, reaching out to catch my shoulders again, "there *is no sickness*. Wolf Ridge isn't sick. People don't have to be from here to do bad things. I know sometimes it's easy to want to place blame—"

"I'm not just placing blame, Dad! I'm not just grieving, or desperate for something to point my finger at, or whatever other bullshit that therapist in the city tried to feed you about me! This is *real*. And I know you know it. I found the articles. I found the one you kept about this town, and what happens every November."

My dad's mouth dropped into a hard frown, and I could see him trying to choose his next words carefully. He started to speak once, then stopped and tried again.

"I wanted something to blame, too, Wyatt. It's normal when you're grieving. I didn't keep those articles because I believed a town-wide sickness was to blame for what happened to your mom. I kept them because I was hurting and searching for an answer. And at the time, any answer would have done."

I chewed hard on the inside of my lip, my arms crossed tight over my chest. I was unsure exactly what I was trying to protect myself from, but while my Dad spoke, a little voice somewhere kept whispering, *the truth*.

The ghosts upstairs were quiet. We stood and stared at each other, neither of us any closer to understanding what had happened than we'd been ten minutes earlier, and neither of us any more comfortable with not knowing. We may have been in pieces, but we were more than the sum of them. We had to be. Otherwise, what did we have left but the pain?

"I'm not going to pretend that what happened to us is at all normal. I won't lie to you and say you'll eventually get over it, because I don't know, Wyatt—maybe you won't. Maybe neither of us will. But I don't think it's necessarily a bad thing that you're having trouble accepting that a human being is capable of doing what someone did to Mom. Maybe it means you aren't totally jaded yet."

I wanted to be angry. I wanted to boil over, ignite the gasoline in my veins, and give myself permission to feel what I needed to feel. I wanted to scream. I wanted to claw and kick and scream and burn the entire town down to splinters and ashes.

"Maybe it means the world hasn't ruined you. And damn it, Wyatt, I wish I could just tell you that things will get better, that there are still good people out there, but I know that isn't the answer you're looking for. Baby, I'm not sure you'll ever find the answer you're looking for."

I needed the Wyatt with the sharp edges. But all I had was the Wyatt I thought I'd rinsed myself clean of the morning after Cash ransacked me, stole all the peace from my body.

I crumpled. I wasn't diamond tough. I was made of matchsticks. At any moment, I could be reduced to ash.

Or maybe I already had been.

The next day at school, there was a moment of silence to mark the first anniversary of Kristen Daniels's death. A group of Kristen's beautiful girlfriends—the Kristenettes, as Cash so fondly called them—tearfully handed out flyers at lunch for the candlelight vigil they had organized for that night, to be held on the football field.

"We want to spread awareness of this issue and try to make sure something like this doesn't happen again," one of them explained as she stood beside my table, stack of flyers held against the front of the black skater dress she wore. I knew their names but tended to get them all mixed up. Christina? Ashlyn? Genevieve? She and the rest of her morose band of blond sisters were all dressed like they'd just arrived from a funeral. One of them even had a black veil fascinator pinned in her hair. The display felt gratuitous, but it wasn't their fault. Some people's need for sympathy was just insatiable.

"What issue, exactly?" Quinn asked, setting her can of diet soda down, turning toward the funeral brigade that had gathered beside our table.

"Oh, um." The girls exchanged looks. "Suicide."

"Oh my god," Quinn exclaimed, pressing a hand to the center of her chest, feigning emotion. "Thank you so much. Thank you for taking it upon yourselves to bring an end to teen suicide by handing out tea lights in paper cups in the middle of a high school football field. I was really, really starting to panic about what we were going to do about this tragic epidemic."

Christina-Ashlyn-Genevieve glowered at Quinn. She smacked a flyer down on the end of the table, and the girls walked off in a tight flock, moving on to the next table.

"Was that entirely necessary?" I asked Quinn, picking up the flyer and looking it over.

Quinn rolled her eyes and took another sip of her soda.

"Their bullshit theatrics aren't necessary, so I think we can call it even." She paused, watching me examine the flyer. "You can't be considering going."

I shrugged. "I don't know."

"Did you even really know Kristen? I think she was just one of those girls everyone knew *of* but didn't really *know*, unless you were one of those living mannequins in her fan club." Quinn nodded toward the girls, now gathered around the next table over like a bunch of grief carolers. I thought of tenth grade, when everyone acted like Kristen deserved a medal for inviting some of the less popular girls to her birthday party. And then, how when some of them showed up, her friends teased them and made them feel unwelcome until they left. Kristen hadn't done anything to stop them. I remembered telling Cash what a bitch she was after that, but now, the only way I pictured Kristen was in her truck, driving it off the bluff. I could only ever wonder how long she'd been that broken.

"I didn't really know her, no, but it's a small town. Are any of us really complete strangers?" I set the flyer down, sliding it across the table to her.

She was studying me, one eyebrow raised, like I'd just spoken to her in Swedish.

"Well, *you* seem a bit like a complete stranger at the moment. Since when do you buy into the public displays of narcissism the bitches of the social elite put on for each other?"

"If I went, it wouldn't be for them," I told her. "It would be for Kristen. Maybe I didn't *know* her know her, but this month really fucking blows, Quinn. And not just for me."

She reached across the table and took my hand in both of hers.

"Sorry, Wy. If you wanna go to the vigil thing, I'll go with you. Unless you're going with your betrothed—I mean, your project partner. Or Cash. Hey, where's he been? I haven't even seen him in school this week at all. Not that I'm complaining. I've gotten more face time with you than usual without Cash constantly kidnapping you."

When she spoke his name, my mind began to tune her out. My ears rang, fuzzy, as she went on, the searing start of an oncoming migraine at the reminder that it had been days since I had seen Cash. And that the last time I had seen him, he had been climbing off of me, leaving me alone on his bed and slamming the front door behind him. I tensed, the yellowing bruises under my clothes suddenly aching like they were fresh.

"Hey. Wyatt." Quinn snapped her fingers in front of my face, and all at once, the static in my head went silent.

"Sorry," I mumbled quickly, pulling the sleeves of my sweatshirt down over my hands, gripping the fabric tightly.

"Speaking of your betrothed," Quinn said, her eyes on something over my shoulder.

I turned around to see Porter entering the lunchroom, flanked on either side by a handful of guys from the track team. I tried to turn back around before he noticed me looking, but Porter grinned the moment he saw me and headed in my direction. I looked at Quinn, who was suddenly gathering up her things.

"Wait, where are you going?" I pleaded, and she laughed at me.

"Forgot about this thing I have to do. You know. That thing," she said as Porter came up beside our table. I clenched my jaw and widened my eyes at her, but she only shouldered her bag and waggled her fingers at me, backing away and eventually turning to walk off.

Porter slid into the seat Quinn had just vacated, smiling at me. I took a sip of cold coffee left over from that morning just to busy myself.

"Subtlety isn't her strong suit, is it?" he asked, reaching over to pluck an M&M from the bag in front of me.

"Quinn? Conspicuous? Never." I smacked his hand away when he reached for more candy. He only grinned and turned his attention to the flyer on the table, pulling it toward him and reading it over. I felt the corners of my lips begin to turn down, and I caught the bottom one between my teeth.

"I think I'm going," I told him, my voice involuntarily going softer. "If you want to go, you wouldn't have to do it alone."

Porter nodded slowly, his eyes still on the flyer.

"Yeah. Yeah, I think I do want to go." He looked up at me. "Thanks."

I offered him a small smile, then slid the package of M&Ms across the table to him, earning me a smile in return. I could feel eyes on us from all directions, but the longer we sat there, sharing peanut M&Ms and talking about how badly we'd done on the calc quiz, the less I noticed anyone else in the lunchroom. By the time the bell rang, we may as well have been completely alone, two kids somehow finding safety in each other, even when the town we lived in was determined to draw blood.

16.

As I walked out of school that afternoon, I put my earbuds in, turning on the playlist I had specially crafted for the days I felt emptied out. There was something almost delicious about sadness; even when it hurt, I still had this strange urge to feed it. I fed mine with music, the sorts of songs that reached into the center of me and gripped tight. This playlist, though, was one I'd made in direct response to Cash trying to take what wasn't his. As I pushed through the front doors, I was immersed in a ballad crooning *I hope you choke in your sleep* when I saw Cash standing in the spot where Quinn usually waited for me, hands in his pockets.

My steps slowed, and I pulled my earbuds out, shoving them into the pocket of my jacket. I approached him slowly, like I was expecting to step on a land mine if I got too close. He watched me, chin ducked, looking up through his eyelashes, that swath of hair over one eye.

I took a deep breath and came to a stop a safe distance from him, eyeing him like he was a wild animal, waiting for some kind of signal that it was safe to approach him.

He finally spoke. "Can we talk?"

"Okay," I answered, but I made no move to get closer.

"Can we go out to the lake?"

"We can talk right here." I glanced around, making sure that the stream of students coming from the doors was still steady.

Cash pressed his lips together, then nodded.

"I've been wanting to call and tell you I'm so—"

I cut him off. "If you're about to apologize, don't." I clenched my hands into fists inside my jacket pockets. "I'm really not interested in hearing it."

"Well, I need to say it," he said, taking a step closer to me. I countered by taking one step back. His frown deepened, but I fought to keep my face blank. I knew he could read me, and I didn't want to give him the satisfaction of knowing how deeply the sound of his voice knifed through me. It was taking everything I had not to follow him to his truck, to let him take me out of town, to lean against him on the ride, to roll the truck windows down and listen to him sing along with old Dashboard Confessional songs.

Wanting to be close to him was involuntary. Muscle memory demanded my arm be linked through his as we walked across the football field in the middle of the night. I was way better at needing him than I was at staying away, even as the bruises he'd left were still healing under my clothes.

He was my drug. I was constantly jonesing for another hit.

"I don't know what got into me. I really don't. I want to blame it on being afraid of losing you, but I know you won't buy that."

I let out an incredulous laugh, shaking my head at him.

"Afraid of losing me? What are you afraid of losing, Cash? I'm not yours. We are not each other's. We never were. You've always made that very, very clear."

"So we didn't have some kind of label," he argued. "Does that really mean I can't be afraid of losing you?"

Looking at him was weakening my resistance. It was unfair how he could break me without even trying. I tried to force myself to think about what he'd done—to focus on the black of his eyes as he stole the last few pieces of me that weren't broken yet.

"It must be nice," I finally said, opening my eyes.

"What?"

"Must be nice to only just now feel like you've lost something, because it has only just now started to matter to you."

"Wyatt—"

"No, Cash. I can't anymore." I took my hands from my pockets to show him my open, empty palms. "I literally have nothing left to give you anymore. You took *everything* from me. What else do you want? Seriously. All I've ever tried to do is give you what you want, to do whatever it took to make you see me. But now I'm out of things to give, and it still wasn't enough."

He bridged the space between us with a few quick strides and reached for me, trying to pull me into his arms, but I knew this game too well. I knew the rules, and I was so tired of playing by them. This was the part where I was supposed to give in and cry into his shoulder and hold him tightly and go back to worshipping in the church of Cash Peters, but I wasn't going to do that this time. After what he'd done, everything had changed. I pushed back against him, fending off his embrace.

"No. Stop it," I said, surprised at my own calm, but he persisted.

"Wyatt. Please."

Cedarwood. Bergamot. I felt my edges softening, the razor blades under my skin starting to dull. I clenched my teeth. Bit the inside of my lip until I tasted blood.

"Listen to me when I fucking say no this time, Cash!"

I shoved him away from me, the volume of my voice making the kids around us grow quiet and turn, watching. In the few seconds I spent trying to get my pulse back to a normal rate, it felt like decades went by with everyone watching me, waiting to see what I would do next.

And then my tear-blurred view of Cash was blocked by the back of a black moto jacket.

"Everything okay here, Wyatt?"

Porter was speaking to me but staring at Cash, barely a foot between their bodies. I stepped back and quickly folded my arms over my chest. Porter and Cash were locked in a stare that may have frozen the ground under our feet if it were any icier.

"Yeah," I heard myself answer after a moment that felt like an hour. "Fine."

I watched the two of them, scared of what the fallout might look like when a full year of unsatiated anger finally came to a head—and of course, it would be my fault. But Porter just nodded a little, his eyes never leaving Cash's even as he spoke to me.

"Good."

Another tense beat passed before Porter finally looked away, turning his eyes to me instead. They softened. He touched a hand to my back, guiding me away. He tossed one more look over his shoulder at Cash before he wrapped his arm around me and walked me out to the parking lot.

I wasn't sure if I felt grateful or embarrassed. I'd spent so many years wanting to belong to someone, but when someone finally tried to claim me, I resisted. I couldn't decide anymore if I wanted to be anyone else's. I could hardly decide if I wanted to belong to myself. I hadn't been a very good caretaker so far. But as we walked to Porter's Jeep, I tried to focus on untangling the mess of thoughts racing through my head.

I climbed into Porter's passenger seat on autopilot, buckling in as he backed out of his space.

"Are you okay?"

His voice pulled me out of the depths of my own head, and I looked over at him as if only just noticing he was there.

"Yeah," I answered automatically.

"It really didn't look like you were okay, Wyatt."

I looked out the window. Tightened my grip on the ends on my sleeves, fingertips pressed into my palms. There was some part of me that wanted to tell Porter what had happened, to let him see the crime scene that was my body, to show him all the spent shell casings rattling around inside my chest. But there was another part of me—a stronger part—that wanted to keep all of it to myself, to keep letting it eat me alive from the inside. Like if I let it out, it might hurt someone else.

I pulled my phone from my pocket and plugged it into the Jeep's auxiliary cord. Porter glanced at me as he drove, and I turned on one of my playlists. This wasn't one I'd made for Cash. It was the one I'd made the afternoon after kissing Porter in the barn, full of songs that hung in the air like a warm haze, each note lingering and lingering. Lana Del Rey. James Bay. Hozier. Allman Brown. But the first song that came on when I pressed shuffle was Ryan Adams's cover of Taylor Swift's "This Love," and from the corner of my eye, I saw a smile brighten Porter's face as the sound filled the car.

He reached over and turned up the volume, and I didn't know where we were going, but Porter didn't seem to either, so we just sank into the sound together as we took the Parkway to the river and followed its winding curves until its currents seemed to sweep away whatever heaviness I'd brought with me. And then Porter reached over and held my hand, and he didn't ask anything of me, didn't expect anything, and for that little while, I forgot about the sickness and the suspect and Kristen Daniels and Cash and what was under my clothes. Even as every instinct I had was telling me not to trust the safety I found in Porter, for a while I settled into the peace of my little refuge, into the scent of Porter and the gentle melodies of love songs.

By the time we got back to the school for the vigil, there was already a steady stream of people making their way from the parking lot to the football field. The procession to the gate was a quiet one. Girls held hands and linked arms, walking close together in groups of two and three. Boys walked with their hands in their pockets. Even though it had been a year, and even though Kristen Daniels certainly wasn't our town's only loss of a young life in recent history, the atmosphere still felt undeniably heavy, a tangible kind of sadness that I didn't know what to do with as I walked with Porter toward the field.

Quinn met us at the gate and hooked her arm through mine, keeping me against her side as we walked in. A few girls were handing out candles in plastic holders, and the three of us each took one before making our way to the center of the field. The lights were off, and people were gathering in a wide circle, passing around lighters and matches to light their candles. The soft glow of candlelight lit the faces of people I knew and people I didn't, of friends from grade school and strangers from other towns. There was something about grief that was so universal that even the mean girls and burnouts and football players were standing shoulder-to-shoulder, touching wick to wick to pass along the light.

Porter stood quietly to my right, his eyes fixed straight ahead. I wound my arm around his waist, giving his body a gentle squeeze, a silent reminder that he wasn't there alone, wasn't feeling what he was feeling by himself. I knew what it felt like to think you were alone in your own personal brand of darkness, specially curated to break you down in the worst way. I knew too well about ghosts and bedroom tombs and photograph shrines and waking up to a blissful half moment of forgetting it all, only to remember it again, the pain suddenly brand new and ancient all at once.

I felt Porter's hand on the small of my back, felt his fingers curl lightly against my jacket. Near the center of the circle, someone was lightly strumming an acoustic guitar. Through a gap in the crowd, I could see a blown-up photo of Kristen resting on a stand and lit by more candles. The whole thing felt like an attempt to dress a wound that was still bleeding. We were all just looking for answers to questions we didn't even know how to ask.

One of the girls who had organized the vigil wheeled out a cart with a projector on it, and I noticed a few of the other girls putting up a screen. A couple of the football players were setting up a speaker and a microphone; what I had thought might be a modest, quiet gathering was beginning to take on the shape of the grief spectacle Quinn had predicted. Beside me, she sighed.

Someone turned the projector on, and Kristen's laughing face illuminated the screen in a soft, eerie glow of blond hair and straight teeth.

Christina-Ashlyn-Genevieve stepped up to the microphone, still clad in the same black skater dress she'd had on at lunch under a cropped black peacoat and a pair of black gloves. Her lips were perfectly painted a deep bloodred.

"Thank you all for coming tonight. Kristen would have been so happy to see so many friends coming together."

I felt Porter tense and shift beside me. On my other side, Quinn let out another sigh. Whatever warmth we had been feeling about the event was starting to freeze over. On the screen, a slideshow moved slowly through a series of photos of Kristen—as a child, pink ribbons tied at the ends of two blond braids; in middle school with braces, gangly arms hooked around the shoulders of smaller versions of Christina-Ashlyn-Genevieve. And then, beautiful and seventeen, just a few weeks before she died, tall and thin with waves of honey blond hanging past her shoulders, her body tucked perfectly into Porter's side. His hair was carefully disheveled, that one brown curl dropping over his eyes. White T-shirt snug around his torso, arms still summer-bronzed and wound around Kristen's waist. She wasn't flashing those bright white teeth at the camera, but up at Porter, the two of them caught in each other's eyes, the moment immortalized and now casting a cold glow over the people gathered on the football field.

I let my arm drop away from Porter. I folded my arms over my chest instead, shrinking up into the protective stance I defaulted to when I felt threatened—this time by a dead girl who was likely nothing more than bones in a box by now, a broken corpse buried beneath layers of flowers and notes and half-melted candles left by the people who loved her. But in that moment, I hated her. All at once, I was a year younger, watching people continue to cry over Kristen Daniels driving her truck over a cliff while my mother's killer went free.

The razor blades under my skin had picked an unfortunate time to resurface. Porter must have noticed, because I could feel his eyes on the side of my face, even while mine stayed fixed on the picture of the two of them.

Was I jealous of a dead girl for having once been close to Porter? Or was I just jealous of her for being dead?

Girls were taking turns at the microphone, gushing about how perfectwonderfulamazingbeautiful Kristen was, but they faded into a blur of long hair and black dresses, their voices drowned out by the ringing in my ears. I closed my eyes to drown it all out, but when I did, I saw the blood-soaked carpet in the upstairs hallway, felt it under my feet, felt it thick and wet on my hands.

The sound of a sudden collective gasp made me open my eyes again.

I looked around to see a crowd of open-mouthed, slack-jawed friends and strangers, wide eyes all fixed on the projector screen. It was like everyone had frozen in place, doomed to stand there and grieve a girl they only half knew until the end of time. But then I saw what they were looking at and pulled my own breath sharply into my lungs, the air cold enough to sting on its way in.

On the screen was Kristen—sprawled across a bed, skirt pulled down to her knees, shirt pushed up to her throat, body naked and bare and exposed. The slideshow cycled through all the photos of her that someone had taken at that party the summer before, interspersed with photos of Kristen grinning and happy. A smiling photo of Kristen's fifteenth birthday, then a photo of her undressed, passed out on the bed.

Girls were trying desperately to turn it off, fumbling with the laptop and projector with shaking hands and shrill voices, too startled and terrified to think to just shut the laptop. The rest of us stood completely still, unable to look away. It felt like watching someone drown and not jumping in after them, just staring, paralyzed, as they thrashed and begged for help.

The photos flashed angrily on the screen in a horrible loop, a skipping record caught on a haunting chorus. People were dissolving into whispers, hands covering mouths, palms pressed to foreheads. We were all equal parts helpless and guilty—we were horrified, but also sickeningly enthralled, drawn to the images like moths to a flame.

I grabbed Porter's arm, trying to pull him away, my gut instinct telling me to get him out of there. Or maybe it was me who really needed to get away. Everything was happening both in slow motion and at full speed, and the ringing in my ears was picking up again. Porter gave in to my urging, stepping back to follow me off the field. And then the slideshow came to a sudden stop. The images of Kristen's naked body were replaced with new ones—Lawson's Bluff, a mangled mess of steel and glass, the blood-spattered spiderweb in the windshield of her truck.

The last image stayed on the screen for only a few seconds before the girls finally managed to shut the whole thing down. Someone finally got the sense to run up and slam the laptop shut. One of the football players stood down the field, gripping an extension cord with shaking hands as he took deep, fast breaths. The girls at the microphone had dissolved into sobs, huddled together in a mass of shuddering shoulders and running mascara.

"What the fuck!" one of them shrieked, her voice like a starter pistol signaling me to turn and head in the opposite direction. Porter and Quinn both followed, all of us silent aside from the sound of our hurried footsteps. Once we reached the parking lot, I pulled open the passenger door of Porter's Jeep. I could still hear the sobs and shouts from the girls on the field.

We sat in the Jeep outside my house, silence wrapped around us. It gripped so tightly I heard myself gasp, the sound cutting through the space between us. Whenever I closed my eyes, I saw Kristen naked. Saw her cracked and spiderwebbed like the glass in her windshield, splashed with blood. Saw the blame laid on all of us who had looked, a garish neon sign behind my closed eyes.

"I know it was Cash. No one else would do something like this."

My own voice startled me. Beside me, Porter didn't look up from the steering wheel, though I could sense the sudden way his breaths deepened. There was a tension between our bodies, a thickness I couldn't bring myself to reach across. It was like I could feel him simultaneously unraveling and tightening every string that was holding him together.

"Even if it was, he isn't wrong. Some of us there tonight were to blame."

I barely recognized Porter's voice. It was a weak, edgeless version of its usual self, sounding miles away rather than inches. I finally looked at him. Reached across the space between us and let my fingertips brush his wrist. He shifted, body turning toward the door and away from me. I pulled my hand back into my lap, fingertips seared from the iciness of his rejection, but I kept my eyes on him. His face was a mix of frustration and pain, and both hands lifted to grip the steering wheel, knuckles going white. I'd never seen him so close to losing himself. I'd never seen so many deep cracks in his sturdy, steadfast exterior.

"What do you mean?" I asked softly. "What do you mean, some of us were to blame?"

Porter slammed one tightly balled fist hard against the steering wheel, sending a shock through me. I inched toward the passenger door, some force pinning me there, some thick, tangible fear of seeing him so broken. Of watching every pin holding him together start to come loose, one by one.

"God damn it, Wyatt."

The soft, melting edges of his voice didn't match the sharpness of his words. My throat tightened. He wouldn't look at me, his eyes fixed on the center of the steering wheel. And when he closed them, I saw a tear fall down his cheek.

"This…" He nodded once, clenching his fist against the wheel again. "This is on me."

It was like watching a clock trying to explain time—something attempting to make sense of its own existence. And I was just trying to put the pieces together in a way that didn't hurt, in a way that didn't color Porter *bad*, shaded in with the same darkness Cash carried. I was so fucking *tired* of making peace with darkness. Of letting it sit beside me and take up space.

I shook my head. I wasn't going to let him do it. I wasn't going to allow him to scratch himself out with black marker in my mind.

"No. Porter, no. You didn't do it. She didn't do it because of you. She was sick, she needed help, she—"

"Wyatt."

"—she was just hurting, and she—"

"*Wyatt!*"

The crack of his voice in the small space of the Jeep shook me. Pinned me against the passenger door. I didn't notice the painfully tight grip I had on the door handle until all five of my fingers suddenly ached.

I was shaking my head, closing my eyes, thinking of just days before, when he had promised me Cash's hatred of him was undeserved. I could feel him about to hand himself over to me, sealed up like evidence, right alongside those photos of Kristen's naked body.

"No," I said out loud. Swallowed a mouthful of pins and needles. "No."

"Yes." He finally looked at me. I tore my eyes from his right away, like I was afraid I'd have to believe it if I kept looking at him, like I'd see the truth and knew it would break me, leave behind only ashes.

"I was drunk. I was mad. She'd been distant for weeks, nitpicking everything I did, so concerned with how she looked to other people that it felt like I was just a puppet she'd sat beside her to complete her perfect portrait. So I went upstairs to confront her, to tell her I was sick of it, 'cause I was drunk and had all this liquid courage telling me to just do it. And then I found her in the bedroom, half undressed and passed out. And I..."

I heard his breath catch. Heard the tremble in his voice get more severe. I made myself look at him, saw his bottom lip visibly quiver while he searched for the words to explain what had happened next. But we both already knew. Even in his silence, he told me everything. And while we both sat there in all that knowing, I closed my eyes.

"I just left her there. I didn't wake her up, didn't fix her clothes. Didn't help her or protect her."

I opened my eyes again. Heard Porter sniffle and clear his throat, and then he sat up a little straighter.

"I woke up the next day, and my phone was blowing up. Someone had sent the photos to me and a bunch of other people, and someone had posted them online. And I did *nothing*. Said *nothing.* Like she'd deserved it or something. And that was it. We broke up, and a few months later…"

His voice trailed off. I watched him wrap both hands around the steering wheel again, tightening and releasing his grip a few times.

"I never told her. I never fucking told her. And when she came to me about it because she didn't know what to do, I told her to *ignore it.*"

The quiet laugh that came out of him sent a shudder through the center of me. I looked at my lap. Tugged my sleeves down over my hands.

"I'm sorry, Wyatt. I lied. Cash thinks I took those photos, and even though I didn't, I could have *stopped* it. I've spent the last year lying to myself and everyone else about what happened and why it happened, to the point where…now, lying about it feels more like telling the truth."

I shook my head, lifting my hand from my lap, trying to hush him. I wanted him to stop. I didn't want to hear any more. Whatever he said only made everything else feel that much heavier, that much more real, that much more like something I couldn't explain away with an imagined sickness.

"You didn't take those pictures and send them around. And you didn't drive her car off that bluff. You fucked up, but you didn't make her do it. Besides," I said, grabbing my bag from the floor and opening the passenger door, "none of us are fucking innocent."

"Wyatt—"

"It's fine, Porter. Go home. I'll see you tomorrow."

And while I slammed the Jeep door shut and jogged up to the front door, I could feel him watching me. But I waited until I got up to my room before I collapsed in a heap against my door and cried until my chest ached.

17.

I woke up the next morning to twelve missed text messages, all from Porter. From the time stamps on the texts, it was clear he'd never gone to sleep. And from the texts themselves, it was clear he was trying pretty desperately to pretend the night before hadn't happened. All the messages were about the party we were throwing that night—Porter asking about decorations and whether I thought we should put signs out on the Parkway and if I thought balloons and party poppers were too much. I scrolled through the messages while I lay in bed, listening to the sounds of Dad downstairs in the kitchen—the clink of the coffeepot, the cabinet where we kept the mugs thudding closed.

I almost clicked off my phone and curled back up to sleep more, the rare peace and comfort of Dad's morning noises making me sigh with sleepiness, until I saw one more name at the bottom of the list of missed text messages.

Cash.

Porter Dawes is a liar.

The night before came back in sudden, harsh flashes—the sound of Porter's voice as he told me the truth, how it felt like hands wrapping around my throat. Like a swift kick to the gut, a painful, relentless reminder that everyone I thought I could trust was capable of cruelty, of violence. But I was still so desperate for answers, for proof that wasn't the only reason for all the shit that happened in our town.

I tossed my phone to the other side of my bed and left it behind as I went downstairs, greeted halfway by the smell of my favorite dark roast coffee brewing. I followed the scent into the kitchen, where my dad was spooning sugar into two mugs on the counter.

"She lives!" he said with a grin. "You didn't wake me when you got home. What happened at the thing last night?"

"Just your standard giant grief spectacle," I said, getting the half-and-half out of the fridge. "But it kind of went up in flames."

"Well, that explains the email from Principal Harris we all got this morning. Are you okay, though?"

"Yeah, Dad, I'm fine." I offered him a smile, and he gave me one back before he touched the cold bottle of cream to the back of my neck on his way to the fridge. I jumped and swatted him away. Again, despite the world practically burning down around us, we ignored the flames and pretended our lungs weren't full of smoke. If acting like things were fine was our only defense against the fact that they weren't, we'd pretend until it killed us.

"So, I've got this thing tonight," I started, trying to craft a valid excuse for inevitably being out all night. "It's technically for school. For a project. We have to film a scene from a book, and we're doing it tonight."

"We?" Dad raised both eyebrows at me.

"Porter Dawes and me."

"Is this what you guys have been working on after school?"

"Yeah, Mr. Vaughn paired us up. Otherwise, I'd probably be partnered with Quinn, who always does the absolute bare minimum."

He was looking at me with a skeptical half smile, but finally, he nodded, then took a sip of his coffee.

"All right. But if for whatever reason this school project turns into drinking, I want you to text me for a ride home. I don't want you getting in the car with anyone who's been drinking. You know, while working on your school project."

I rolled my eyes, already turning to walk out of the kitchen.

"Yeah, Dad, it's gonna be a total rager."

And part of me hoped I wasn't kidding.

Upstairs, my laptop dinged with a new email. I opened it and saw Jennifer's name in my inbox, the subject line in all lowercase letters: found something.

In the email, there was a scanned image of a newspaper article, dated November 29, 1992.

LAMOILLE COUNTY TOWN SEES
THIRD DEATH THIS MONTH

The town of Wolf Ridge, situated in central Lamoille County, has seen three suspicious deaths this month alone, surpassing yearly averages for the area. The first death occurred on November 1, when nineteen-year-old Vincent Clay died by suicide. The second death occurred November 13, when an eight-year-old boy was killed in a hit-and-run while riding his bike. The third death, that of twenty-three-year-old Georgia Vaughn, occurred November 21. Vaughn was found dead in her parents' home in Wolf Ridge, apparently having been strangled.

I read and reread the name of the third victim until my eyes blurred. I closed them, trying to do the math in my head. Vaughn. Twenty-three in 1992. Could she have been Mr. Vaughn's mother? Had he ever mentioned his mother, or lack of one? Had he been tied to Wolf Ridge all along?

I skimmed the rest of the article, which was just a discussion of the abnormality of three deaths happening in one month in such a small town in an otherwise low-crime county. But that name kept circulating in my mind.

Below the scan of the article was more from Jennifer:

You could be on to something. Let's talk more.

––––––––––

Porter's online invitation had instructed everyone to dress up in their best twenties garb, so I wasn't at all surprised to find Quinn in her bedroom that evening, dressed up in the flapper costume she'd worn two Halloweens ago: a short, dark red dress with a low neckline and an open back.

"Won't you be freezing?" I said, sitting on the edge of her bed. "This thing is technically outside, you know."

"It's in a building with a hundred other people. I think it'll be pretty warm. Speaking of, you really need to lose that cardigan, Nancy Drew."

I pulled my sweater tighter around myself, rolling my eyes at her. After I'd put on the dress I'd chosen to wear to the party, a sudden stab of self-consciousness had made me grab the cardigan. I was wearing it half because I was slightly embarrassed to let anyone see me in a dress that short and tight and half because of the light remnants of the bruises on my wrists.

Quinn's bedroom felt as familiar as my own. Since we'd met in grade school, we'd spent every weekend we could in her bedroom or mine, sharing bowls of popcorn and sneaking out the window once we hit high school. We'd sat outside on the roof, passing joints back and forth, while Quinn talked about the boys who constantly vied for her attention and I stayed mired in my hopeless attachment to a boy who would never love me the way I loved him.

Quinn draped a few long strands of fake pearls around her neck, and I watched as she leaned into her floor-length mirror, carefully crafting the perfect cat eye with glittery black eyeliner. She looked like a dream. Her dress looked like it had been made just for her, hair falling in loose curls over her shoulders. She pulled a black band down around her forehead, a feather attached to one side. Then she turned around to face me, pressing her lips together in a glossy red pout.

"You look like an extra in Baz Luhrmann's *Gatsby* remake," I said, looking her over. "I'm pretty impressed."

"Here," she said, going over to her vanity and digging through the basket of hair accessories. She pulled out a dark red satin rose and a few hairpins. Before I could protest, she gathered a lock of my hair, twisted it, and pinned the rose just above my temple. She grinned down at me once she had finished.

"And..." Quinn snatched up the tube of lipstick she'd used, popping off the cap and applying a careful, smooth layer to my lips.

"Hellfire Red." She showed me the name of the shade on the end of the tube.

I stood and stepped over to the mirror, hardly recognizing the girl I saw. Dark hair down instead of tied up, that satin rose drawing attention to the thick liner perfectly drawn on my top lids, accented with a sprinkle of gold glitter, thanks to Quinn's makeup drawer being as bottomless as Mary Poppins's carpetbag. I couldn't remember the last time I'd worn anything more than a smudgy layer of mascara. The dark circles under my eyes were usually the only color on my otherwise-pale face. But the girl standing there in the mirror? She was a dark-haired pinup hidden under a cardigan. Swap that cardigan for some nameless bad boy's leather jacket, and she could swing her hips up to just about anyone and say through cigarette smoke, *Eat your heart out.*

Outside, the sun was disappearing behind the houses across the street. Quinn spritzed a cloud of Chanel perfume—a bottle she'd stolen from someone's mother's bathroom at a party—and walked through it.

"Ready?" she asked, already halfway out of the bedroom door.

In my hand, my phone lit up with a text from Porter. My heart simultaneously swelled and sank.

your soirée awaits, madame.

A steady stream of cars were turning off the Parkway down the dirt road that led to the barn. I'd promised Porter I wouldn't show up early to help him finish setting up, despite the fact that letting him take control of our project-turned-party was making me anxious. He'd wanted to surprise me with the finished product, and every bit of excitement that sparked in me also brought on twice as much anxiety. The disaster that was the vigil for Kristen was a fresh, bleeding wound for most of the people at school, and I thought that the possibility of another big gathering going up in flames might keep people from showing up.

I was *very* wrong.

I could hear the music pulsing from the barn before it was even in sight. Rows of haphazardly parked cars lined the dirt road. Groups of girls in flapper dresses and masquerade masks followed groups of boys in blazers and fedoras toward the barn. Quinn drove up as close as she could, pulling up right beside Porter's Jeep.

"This is your fucking lit project, Wyatt Green, and I definitely hate you for it," she said as she got out of the car, the colored lights spilling from the open barn doors painting her bare arms and face. Before I could make it all the way around the car to her side, a pair of warm hands caught hold of my waist from behind, a set of lips suddenly against my ear.

"Your face is familiar," Porter said low, his voice sending a wave of goose bumps over the back of my neck. "Were you in the war?"

Despite the lingering ache in my chest from the night before, I grinned, recognizing his admittedly poor attempt at quoting *Gatsby*. I remembered what he'd said about Gatsby and Nick being the real romance in the novel, and my stomach practically backflipped. Quinn was watching us, and I could see her smirking.

"I was," I answered, still not moving, letting Porter hold my waist and letting other people—strangers and not—see him do it.

"I knew I'd seen you before."

Porter's lips dropped to the curve of my neck. The pulse of bass and music and the happy shouts of people inside the barn dissolved like sugar in water. I just couldn't decide if I *was* the water or if I was drowning in it. I slipped out of Porter's reach and turned to face him, Quinn hurrying over to hook her arm through mine.

"You're being a terrible host, leaving your guests alone, Mr. Gatsby," I played along, returning the grin Porter was wearing. Now that I could see him, I noticed his slim-fitting black pants and half-undone white button-up under a pair of black suspenders. His sleeves were loosely rolled up, and that lock of chestnut hair that usually fell over one eye had been smoothed back.

"Are you *kidding* me?" Quinn said as she tugged me along. "Why does he look *that* good? Pretty sure that kind of torture violates the Geneva Convention…"

The Wyatt with the sharp edges would have rolled her eyes, but this Wyatt, the Wyatt with the silly grin and red lipstick, just sank into the strange, relentless freedom of the night—a tight fist suddenly letting go of all the glitter and stardust it was holding. Quinn pulled me toward the open barn door, Porter jogging to catch up. And as I walked inside, whatever else I was holding on to deep in the center of me disappeared— Porter's confession, the vigil, the lingering aches could all be dealt with later. In the barn, Porter's finished product came to life around me like I'd stepped inside a 1920s fever dream.

The lights we'd hung were the absolute least of it. They'd multiplied somehow, the beams practically invisible under thousands of twinkling, glittering bulbs. Tinsel streamers in gold and silver and purple and black draped and dripped from the light strands and beams, occasionally fluttering down onto the crowd of people like metallic snow. I spotted a punch bowl filled with confetti and glitter poppers, and every time someone set one off, the room erupted in shouts and screams that sounded like songs.

I felt so far away from the things that hurt. Wolf Ridge may as well have been a thousand miles behind me.

"What do you think?"

I looked over to see Porter beside me, arms folded as he surveyed his creation. He'd built an entire world, a wonderland I could exist in for the night, where there weren't any ghosts waiting in the dark corners. I thought of the Wyatt who loved Cash Peters. The girl who maybe loved to be sad more than she really loved any person. That girl had no idea this other one was still inside her, silenced by grief and disenchantment.

"I think...this is the first time I'm not the one who did all the work for a group project."

"Oh, Wyatt," Porter said over the music. "You haven't even seen half of it."

Before I could say anything else, Porter disappeared into the crowd. I looked around, recognizing faces lit in colored lights, noticing that even the Kristenettes had shown up—a huddled group of sideswept hair and elbow-length black gloves. For a second, I wondered why those girls would ever show up at a party I was throwing, and then I remembered they weren't there for me. They were there for Porter. This seemingly familiar boy had an entire other life. A life full of pretty girls like Kristen Daniels, parties like this one, expensive cars, track meets. Wolf Ridge may have been small, but everyone seemed to have their own private universes, just streets away from one another but still worlds apart. The party didn't exist in a universe I knew; this was alien territory.

"Okay," Quinn said, beside me again, "you aren't really planning on keeping this on, are you?"

She pulled my cardigan down from my shoulders and off of my arms before I could tell her not to, and a flash of panic lit in my chest. But when I looked down at my bare arms, the darkness that still shadowed my wrists was invisible under the colored lights.

It felt like I was swimming in a current of light and sound, everything happening in slow motion and at light speed all at once. I was edgeless—but this time, in a good way. In the way that let me feel like a part of something rather than standing outside of it.

The up-tempo song that was playing suddenly faded out, replaced by a familiar acoustic ballad. A nervous tingle swept through me, all the way down to my fingertips. The melody was one I recognized from rides in Porter's passenger seat, from the day I'd let him twirl and dip me in this barn like I was the same kind of free he was, even though it felt foreign, like trying to get used to moving without gravity.

The people around me slowly parted, opening a path straight ahead. Porter walked through the crowd, moving toward me and pushing a hand through his hair to smooth it back. He had the sly smile and bashful gaze of a boy in a romantic comedy, coming in at just the right moment and in just the right light to make the whole thing feel like some kind of waking dream.

People paired off around us, winding arms around one another and swaying gently to the music. It felt like a middle school dance and a daydream all at once, and the only thing I could convince my mouth to do was smile.

"I don't remember Gatsby and Nick slow dancing in the novel," I told Porter as he took my hand and moved an arm around my waist, drawing me closer to him.

He just grinned.

"Call it a creative interpretation."

"Not sure Vaughn will buy that one." I felt my heart rattling around inside my chest like a bird in a cage.

"Oh, come on, Wyatt Green," Porter sighed. One corner of his lips pulled up. He leaned his face closer to mine. "You can't honestly still believe I did all this for a class project."

He twirled me out away from his body before I could register that properly, and I was suddenly six years old again, spinning in a Cinderella nightgown and gripping my father's finger. It was a flash of innocence I hadn't even remembered until just that moment, so much of my life before Mom's death having dissolved into ashes. But here was this familiar stranger, creating a world for me where I could be as weightless as a little girl, dancing in the kitchen in a princess nightgown. Here, I wasn't carrying the dull ache of Cash's marks or the still-lingering sting of Porter's admission. Whatever this world was, I wanted to stay in it. I wanted to trust it.

I spun back into Porter's arms.

Glitter and tinsel settled in our hair and on our shoulders.

There was only his hand, low on my back. Only his cheek against mine. I could close my eyes, and we could be anywhere. We could be dancing in the middle of a Paris street. In the tomb of some Egyptian queen. We could be everywhere and nowhere all at once.

We were so far away, I barely heard the screams starting to seep in through the cracks.

Somewhere in the barn, sparks had flown into flames, setting off an eruption of noise and chaos.

The world Porter had built, in all of its gorgeous slow motion, fell around us like a curtain on a stage. We were no longer safe, suddenly back on the ground, that little girl in the princess dress dissolving into ash with one last twirl.

Heat billowed from one corner of the barn as flames climbed up to the rafters, the light strings popping in loud bursts. Tinsel and streamers fell in strings of ember and ash, singeing dress hems and shirtsleeves.

My ears were ringing. They felt clouded, like I was suddenly underwater, despite the impossible heat. I looked up at Porter. He was saying something, his face colorless, eyes watching something over my shoulder. Even from underwater, I heard him saying my name.

Wyatt. Wyatt.

The loud crack of a rafter collapsing brought all the sound back at once, a sharp stab that seemed to pierce me straight through.

There was so much screaming, it drowned out the music,

even though our song had switched to something fast and loud enough to make my rib cage shudder with each pulse of bass. Everything still felt unreal, like whatever was happening was just taking place inside my head, like my feet weren't actually on the ground. Like Porter wasn't actually holding on to me, it wasn't actually November, I wasn't actually in Wolf Ridge, I wasn't actually Wyatt.

Wyatt.

I heard my name again. It was coming from Porter.

"Wyatt. Can you hear me? Come on."

Bodies shoved past my shoulders, sending me stumbling into Porter's grip. I'd been dropped into the center of a war zone. Girls cowered in corners, coughing as the barn filled with black smoke, gloved hands covering their heads. Others ran past us in chains of linked hands and a rush of screams and sobs. Dean and a few other boys from the track team were suddenly around us, trying to usher us toward the open barn doors.

"Wyatt! Let's go!" Porter shouted, fear and urgency blurring the edges of his voice. I started to let the boys guide me out, trying to keep my feet under me as I followed Porter to the doors. But something stopped me like a force field, feet from the door.

"Quinn!" I heard myself scream, but my voice didn't sound like my own. I turned back, pushing past shoulders, searching for a flash of Quinn's blond hair in all the noise and movement.

Porter's tight grip around my wrist tugged me back.

"Wyatt! No. Come on."

I pulled hard, trying to shove him off of me.

"I have to find Quinn!"

The color still hadn't returned to his face. When I said Quinn's name, he went even paler. I remembered the way he'd stared over my shoulder moments before, felt my heart drop out of my chest like a stone into a pond.

I yanked my wrist free and pushed my way farther into the barn, toward the side that had mostly emptied out. I screamed Quinn's name over the music, which now just sounded shrill and unsettling, some sort of sickening soundtrack to that moment.

I emerged from the mass of people trying to get to the door, taking in a deep breath like I'd just come up from underwater, choking on the thickening smoke.

She was there.

Collapsed on the ground like a dropped doll. Red lips parted just slightly. Chest rattling with shallow breaths. Blood was pooling around her head, seeping from a gash left by the fallen rafter, in a heap of splinters beside her.

"Quinn."

I said her name, but the sound of it got swallowed up by the noise and smoke. I knelt beside her and took her face between my hands.

"Quinny. Baby."

I moved my hand around to the back of her neck to lift her, my fingers sweeping through the thick warmth of the blood on her skin. It soaked through my dress as I laid her head in my lap. When I saw the blood on my palms, something ricocheted inside my skull—the sharp smack of a memory I'd forgotten I had.

Standing on the blood-soaked carpet in the hallway. Looking down at my hands, covered in deep red. My mother just feet away, dead and staring at me.

Look what he did to me, she'd said when I dreamed of her. *Look what he did to me.*

18.

Everything came back in fragments.

My mother in the hallway as I stumbled into the house after curfew. The fire I spat at her. Her hushed conversations with Dad behind their bedroom door—*We have to get her away from Cash*. A broken film reel in my head, jumping forward to a procession of suspects that I tried to place in the house, tried to imagine sinking the kitchen knife into my mother's stomach. But none of them fit, and the film reel always played back a faceless body ascending the stairs in my house.

Porter, his smile, lit class.

The vigil, the photos of Kristen casting a sick glow over the crowd of people.

The barn. The party.

I felt both awake and asleep, unable to decide which

memories were real and which I'd made up. I blamed it on the sickness, called it a symptom of November. It shouldn't have surprised me that something I'd tried to find peace and happiness in had gone up in literal flames. No one in Wolf Ridge was safe.

The cops, on the other hand, weren't interested in my stories about the sickness. Sheriff Grant kept Porter and me at the station until the sun peeked in through the high, narrow windows of the office I was sitting in. Every so often, Grant came in and asked the same questions.

Did you see how the fire started?

Do you know if the wiring was faulty?

Did you have permission to use the barn for the party?

He pressed his lips together in a tight line when I gave him the same answers each time.

No.

I didn't.

I have no idea.

They'd let me wash my hands when we got to the station and gave me a jacket to put on over my bare arms, but my dress was still stiff with dried blood. It was still under my fingernails. My palms were still tinted pink. Everything still smelled of smoke—my hair, my clothes. Apparently, I'd been so covered in blood they thought I'd been hurt, too. I remembered hands on me, remembered screaming so loud my voice strained as someone pulled me away from Quinn's side. Remembered the red-and-blue glow against the side of the barn. The heat, so intense I could feel it even from a hundred yards away, watching from the back of an ambulance as the barn burned. Huddled masses of strangers and acquaintances, mascara smeared down faces. Fire engine sirens echoing across the field, bouncing off the tree line.

At some point after we'd gotten to the station, I'd heard my father's voice tear through the building like lightning through a storm cloud. From the room they were holding me in, I could just make out a string of curse words with my name threaded between them.

By the time the sun came up, I was half asleep with my head on my folded arms, hunched over the table in the otherwise-empty room. The light dripped down from the high windows, gray and cold against the side of my face. I played the night over in my head, a broken film reel with some frames missing, others already tarnished by the faultiness of memory.

Twinkling lights.

Black dress.

Hellfire lips.

That song.

Porter's hands.

A blur of noise and smoke and movement.

Broken doll pieces on the ground on the far side of the barn.

My mother—

No. Quinn.

Quinn.

And then the film started to skip and crackle, those frames

riddled with burns. When it refocused, I was back in the empty barn, standing over Quinn's body with my bloody hands out in front of me.

Quinn's eyes snapped open. She grabbed my wrist with one cracked porcelain hand and brought my fingers to the gash on her head, screaming, *Look what he did to me—*

I sat up in my chair so quickly that I nearly fell backward. I gripped the edge of the table, white knuckles stained pink. I counted the wild, banging beats of my heart against my ribs, trying to ground myself, but I felt like a weather vane in a lightning storm. I was pulsing with electricity. There were razor blades trying to move through my veins. Suddenly, the light coming in felt oppressive—a spotlight turned on a crime scene.

The door opened, and Sheriff Grant came in. This time, I got up from my chair. I must have looked half crazed, judging by the way he stared at me and took a step back.

"You have no right to keep me here." I pointed at him, but I saw my hand shake, saw the lingering stain on my fingertip, and shoved it quickly into the pocket of my borrowed jacket.

"Wyatt—"

"Are you charging me with something?"

I surprised us both with the sharp edge in my voice. Grant opened his mouth to speak, then closed it again. He still looked scared of me, and he kept enough space between us that he could duck quickly back out the door if he needed to.

"Not at this time. Although the owner of the barn may wish—"

"Then let me go home."

His answers were all so careful, while my voice cut like a blade. I could tell he was picking his words as if they were all made of glass. Delicately.

"There's some paperwork—"

"My best friend was almost killed, and you're talking about paperwork? No wonder my mother's case is cold."

Grant's shoulders went back as he straightened, clearly bristling at my accusation.

I recognized this girl. This girl had edges, took up space. This girl wore anger like a tattoo, deep and permanent.

Instead of responding, Grant simply stepped aside, leaving the doorway clear. I shrugged the jacket off of my shoulders and tossed it over the back of the chair, my eyes still set on Grant. I couldn't decide if I felt like the prey or the hunter. In the unfriendly light, my bare arms practically glowed, the shadows of leftover bruises suddenly looking darker.

Grant gestured to the open door I was already stepping through, giving me permission I hadn't waited for.

Dad was on a bench near the front entrance. He held his head in his hands, elbows propped on his knees, shoulders heavy with the kind of defeat I hadn't seen him wear in months. Seeing him, the shape he'd taken on, stopped me cold.

"Daddy."

The sound came from me involuntarily. Dad's head shot up, and he was on his feet and bridging the space between us in two strides. He wrapped me up in his arms tightly, but still

I felt like I might dissolve at any moment, wind up a pile of ashes at his feet. His tight embrace helped me keep my shape. He held on to me and walked me out of the station to his car, wordless, but I wasn't sure I would have been able to hear him over the screaming in my ears, even if he'd spoken. I couldn't even tell whether it was coming from inside my head or not.

At home, the ghosts were quiet. The whole house felt like a tomb. We sat silently inside like it was a funeral and we were too exhausted to deliver the eulogy. I spent the next few hours sitting so still on the sofa that I became part of the furniture, just another throw pillow or armchair taking up space. Dad sat on the opposite end of the sofa, eventually falling asleep. His breathing mapped the day's descent into afternoon, into evening, when the dingy yellow dusk felt more like darkness.

My head played the fractured film reel on a sickening loop.

Every few moments, my entire body flinched at the vicious roar of fire rattling through my memory.

My phone, which the cops had finally given back to me before we'd left the station, sat on the coffee table. I pressed the home button to wake the screen and saw a series of missed calls and texts, most from Porter.

please answer

i just need to know you're ok

i have to talk to you pls call

My thumb hovered over the call button beside his name. Part of me wanted to hear his voice, but the other part just wanted silence. I shut the screen off. Within a few seconds, it lit up again, phone vibrating in my hand. A photo of Porter I'd taken on one of our afternoons at the barn filled up the screen. I glanced down at my dad, asleep at the other end of the sofa. I wanted to let him stay asleep, where things were hopefully less of a train wreck than real life was, so I tossed the throw blanket off my lap and slipped out the back door. The wood of the back porch was cold, even through my socks. The wind bit at my hands and face. I dragged my thumb across the screen to answer before it could go to voicemail.

"Hey."

"Wyatt. Thank God."

Porter sounded winded, breathless with relief that I'd answered. I waited, pulling my shirtsleeves down into my palms.

"Are you okay?" he asked after a beat of silence. "What did they say to you at the police station?"

"I'm okay," I said, only half believing it. Every time I so much as dozed off on the sofa, I woke to the feeling of flames on my skin, coughing out imaginary smoke. "They just kept asking if I knew about any faulty wiring and whether we had permission to be there."

"Yeah. Me too." I heard him sigh. "I am so sorry, Wyatt."

For some reason, every muscle in my body tensed. I gripped the phone tighter, pressed my lips together, bristling at his words. Apologies felt so toxic now. Hurting, never helping.

"You didn't do this," I said. "You just threw a party."

"Still. Maybe if I hadn't pushed for us to have this big thing—"

"Don't. Don't start with the maybes and what-ifs. Quinn may not wake up. No amount of maybes and what-ifs are going to change that."

Another beat of silence. Wind cut through my light sweater. Cold soaked through my leggings and socks. I sniffled.

"So what do we do, then?" he asked.

"What do you mean?"

"I mean, we have to figure out what happened, don't we? The cops aren't exactly known for their high-quality police work around here."

I'd grown so used to Cash's passive stance on anything even mildly difficult that it was surprising to hear that Porter wanted to do something.

I chewed my lip. Watched the bare limbs of the trees in the backyard shiver.

"I wish I knew what to do," I said. "Where to even start. But I don't. If I did, I would probably know more about my own mom's murder by now."

Porter audibly pulled in a breath. I kept talking before he could say anything.

"Maybe Cash has been right all along, Porter. There is no sickness here. Things are just *bad*. People are just horrible. And there's nothing either of us can do to change that."

Another breath from his end of the line. A pause.

"That's what Cash told you, huh?"

"Ever since his mom killed herself," I answered.

The breath that came from him then was edged with a

laugh, and I felt every inch of me bristle, my readiness to fight for Cash as instinctive as breathing, no matter what he'd done to me. When Porter didn't immediately speak, I felt my pulse quicken again.

"What?" I practically snapped. "What now?"

"I don't want to talk about all this over the phone," Porter said. "Can I come pick you up? Or will you meet me somewhere?"

I looked over my shoulder through the glass of the back door at my dad on the sofa, still asleep. I knew this was probably the first good sleep he'd gotten in weeks.

The trees in the backyard shook. Everything else stood perfectly still.

"I'll come over," I said.

Porter lived just outside Wolf Ridge, a few miles past the barn off the Parkway in a gated subdivision full of sprawling houses on a handful of acres each. All the kids who lived in the subdivision went to school in Wolf Ridge, including Kristen Daniels before she died, but I couldn't remember ever having been inside the gates. Cash and I used to drive past there on our way to the lake. Once, a few months ago, Cash had pulled over across from the entrance, and when I'd asked him what he was doing, he'd just said, "Know why they've got a gate? It isn't to keep people out. It's to keep all their bullshit inside."

The gates were open when I drove up. I'd taken a roundabout route to get there, wanting to avoid the turnoff to the barn, which I knew was blocked with a police barrier. I didn't want to see the yellow crime scene tape hung across the break in the fence like some sick version of a grand opening ribbon.

Dad had been hesitant to let me leave, anxiety blending with the exhaustion on his face. But ultimately he'd relented, making me promise to be careful. He sent a text as I turned off the Parkway and through the gates of Porter's neighborhood.

Be safe. Call if you'll be late.

Porter's house was near the back of the subdivision. His driveway was long, winding uphill before the tree line gave way to the wide, open space of the front yard. His Jeep was parked near the front door, behind his parents' cars. The house looked like a modern take on a log cabin, with a dark-stained wood exterior and wide, bright windows covering almost the entire front facade.

I parked my dad's car behind Porter's Jeep and got out, heading toward the frosted glass double doors that acted as the front entryway. I realized, suddenly, that I probably looked like a wreck. After the frantic shower I'd taken when we got home from the station, I'd thrown on leggings and an oversize sweatshirt that used to be my dad's. I quickly pulled up my wavy, air-dried hair. Just as I reached for the doorbell, one of the double doors swung open.

"Hey, come on in," Porter said, stepping aside to let me move past him.

The foyer had a cathedral ceiling and a staircase leading up to the second floor on either side of the room. Past it, I could see part of the living room and a hall that went all the way to the back of the house, which looked to be yet another wall of windows, covering the backyard in warm light.

Before I could say anything, Porter shut the front door behind me, and then his arms were around me. Some deep, primitive part of me wanted to shove him away out of sheer instinct, but some other part, the one that had iced over since the night before, began to melt into him.

I ended up somewhere in between, with my muscles loosening in his hold but only one hand lifting to grasp a tight handful of his shirt.

His lips touched my temple. The house was quiet around us. We stood there in the foyer for what felt like seconds and years all at once, letting the world keep going without us.

Before my eyes could spill the tears I felt threatening me with a sharp burn in my throat, I pulled back from Porter. I nudged my shoes off and left them beside the others near the door. I followed him through the house, our feet silent on the wood floor of the foyer and the plush white carpet of the stairs. Even though I'd never been there before, I felt like my body was following muscle memory on the way to Porter's bedroom. Even though his parents were there somewhere, the house was quiet, but I still couldn't hear the sound of screams inside my head. My mind, the house, and Porter were all silent.

It wasn't until we were in his bedroom that I remembered why I'd come to Porter's house to begin with.

"So, what couldn't you talk about over the phone?" I asked, turning to him as he shut the door.

My question seemed to catch him off guard. He froze, and I suddenly noticed how exhausted he looked. There were deep circles under his eyes. His hair was sticking out in different directions rather than falling in its usual perfect swoop over one eye. All of a sudden, I was seeing him as he had looked the night before: hands on my shoulders, eyes wide, lips forming the shape of my name although the sound barely reached me over the noise. It already felt like months ago, but somehow it felt like it was also still happening, like we'd never gotten out of that barn.

Porter moved over to his unmade bed and sat down on the edge. He pushed a hand through his wild hair, and it was like I could hear his thoughts, they were so loud. I swallowed back another question and waited.

"There's something I haven't told you about Cash."

Whenever Porter said Cash's name, it always made me catch myself, like when I thought I'd hit the bottom step but there was one more beneath it. I felt the instinct to pull into myself and fought it.

"What about him?"

When Porter didn't answer right away, I stepped over and sank down beside him on the bed, folding my legs under myself and facing him, watching his profile while he gathered his thoughts.

"I didn't tell you the entire story about Kristen. About that party, and why Cash hates me."

I didn't say anything. The film reel in my head skipped and

clicked, and I saw Kristen Daniels, naked and unconscious, sprawled on a stranger's bed.

"There was a reason Cash got so mad about those photos, and why he came after me when Kristen died. It wasn't because he's some upstanding guy who cared just out of the goodness of his heart. He got mad because...he was seeing Kristen. I found out before the party. That's why I left her there—I was mad. I'd been waiting for her to confess, but then I saw them talking at the party, saw him come downstairs not too long before I went up to find her. The photos weren't the reason we broke up. We broke up because she found out I knew and ended it. We broke up, and I assumed you and Cash..."

He trailed off, but I was still stuck back at the beginning of his story, back at *he was seeing Kristen*. I was suddenly at war with myself, one side of me trying to convince the other that Cash had never been mine to begin with, and the other side going up in flames. The lingering bruises under my sweatshirt suddenly felt fresh, aching and deep. The film reel in my head rewound violently, throwing me back into the memory of being in Cash's bed, limp and no longer fighting, staring at his bedroom wall, memorizing the shape of the crack in the drywall from when he'd thrown his fist against it after his mom bled out in the bathtub.

I must have looked as far gone as I was, because Porter's hand was suddenly on my arm, squeezing gently, urging me closer to him.

"I'm sorry. Fuck, I shouldn't have said anything. Not today. How emotionally tone-deaf can I be?"

He was rambling apologies, and I tried to use his words like a life raft to pull me back to the safe shores of his body. Inside, I was gasping for air in white waters. Outside, I was staring at a fixed point on the floor, trying to remember gravity.

I felt my back against Cash's bed again, the weight of his body on mine. The broken glass in his voice. And I wondered about the heart in his chest, how it had been beating just inches from mine while he hurt me. Was it just broken, shattered to the point of being unrecognizable? Or had he just been desperate to claim me because Kristen had so blatantly refused to claim him?

Did rejection make us want to belong so much that we lost sight of who we were? Did pain weaken us to the point where cruelty was the only way we could stay standing? To prove we still felt anything at all?

"Wyatt, I'm sorry. I just couldn't keep the truth from you anymore. I don't wanna be another guy who lies to you. When you said that Cash was always telling you people are inherently horrible, I knew why. It's probably easier for him to think that being shitty is just a human condition. It means he doesn't have to take responsibility for the things he does or do anything to fix them."

I looked at him, finally. I studied his face, those circles under his usually bright eyes, and I lifted my hands to touch him, mapping out his jaw and cheekbones with my fingertips. Porter wasn't perfect, but he was *good*. He was the truth when everyone else, everything else was shrouded in fiction.

Something told me to return the favor. To be honest with him, too.

I took my hands away but kept my eyes on him. I pulled the hem of my sweatshirt up and over my head, his confused expression momentarily disappearing from view until I pulled the fabric free of my body. Underneath, I was bare, my skin pale and exposed, lingering bruises suddenly as bright as Christmas ornaments on a dead tree. The shadows of Cash's greedy touches darkened my arms, my wrists, even my collarbone. The small pink circle of a scar lingered on the inside of my elbow from where I'd once put a lit cigarette out on my skin because I was so desperate to feel something other than emptiness after my mother died.

And when I sat there exposed in front of him, Porter didn't dissolve into weakness, or beg me not to give myself to him, or tell me he wasn't the one who could fix me. He didn't even assume I was asking to be saved. Didn't put his palms up in front of himself, construct a wall around his body and forbid me from entering.

No.

He took my hands gently in his own, his touch so light I had to look down to be sure he was even there at all.

And then he asked, barely a whisper, "Can I?"

I nodded, but the question sounded almost like a foreign language. I was never the one being asked. I was always doing the asking.

Porter ran his fingertips over the bruises, over the scar,

pushed a fallen lock of hair against my shoulder and drew his thumb across the mark on my collarbone. He studied me like a work of art in a museum, one he was determined to understand even though he didn't yet. And I studied him back, watching his face change, hair falling over one eye, the strange familiar boy I was learning and relearning.

Less than twenty-four hours before, we were dancing under a galaxy he'd built for me.

Less than twenty-four hours before, I was staring into his eyes while that galaxy crumbled, while the stars he'd hung for me fell in piles of ash around us.

And now, we were meeting again for the first time, carving out another quiet corner of the universe where we could exist safely.

Porter's face changed again. He looked like he'd suddenly solved an equation he'd been working in his head.

"This isn't..." He trailed off, fingers finding their way to the darkened rings around my wrists. "This isn't from last night."

I shook my head slowly, and it somehow felt like I was admitting it to myself as much as I was to Porter.

Cash had hurt me. Hurt me. Hurt. Me.

Before I could repeat it all back to myself, I felt my shoulders fall. Felt the sharp tightening in my throat just before I began to cry with the ugly, shuddering kind of sobs that seemed to come from the very center of me. I could hardly decide why I was crying. Allowing myself to accept that Cash had hurt me? Quinn's quiet body, hooked up to machines in a hospital bed, closed eyes still speckled with glitter?

Both of those things? Neither?

It must not have mattered to Porter what fresh, bleeding wound was making me cry, because he pulled me against his chest all the same.

"People aren't all bad, Wyatt," Porter whispered into my hair. "You deserve to be able to expect better from people. You *deserve* better."

My body tensed in an involuntary rush of nerves, every instinct I had suddenly telling me to doubt him, to question his motives, to assume that Porter, like everyone else, would only hurt me eventually. I pulled out of his hold, snatched up my sweatshirt and held it against my bare chest, embarrassed.

"Why?" I heard myself croak, the word more like a plea than a question. "Why do I deserve better? You don't even know me, Porter. I don't know you, really. How do you know this isn't *exactly* what I deserve?"

The way his face changed startled me. The softness in his eyes sharpened. His lips went into a thin line, turning down at the corners.

"No, Wyatt," he started, and the slight edge to his voice was already starting to cut into me. "I guess you don't know me. I guess you really have existed on a different plane from me, like you said. But like I said then, *you* did that. *You* chose that. You and Cash chose to separate yourselves from everyone else. So maybe you don't know me. But I know you, Wyatt. I know that when we were in the fifth grade, you punched Julian Smith on the playground for calling Quinn fat. I know that in middle school, your favorite novel was *The Giver*, and I remember the essay you wrote about it, the one that Ms. Linney pinned up on the board. I remember when you dyed your hair purple our freshman year, and when Kristen and her friends teased you about it at lunch, you didn't even look up from the book you were reading, which was *Beloved*. And I remember when you got really close with Cash Peters and started following him around like a kicked puppy. And how you started smoking then and came to school drunk a few times."

As he spoke, I felt my hands start to shake, my grip on my sweatshirt loosening and tightening over and over until my knuckles went white. Something ached right down in the core of me as I listened to him. I both wished he would stop and desperately needed him to keep going.

"And I remember," he continued, his voice suddenly softer, suddenly punctuated with pauses to collect himself, "I remember when your mom died. And I remember sitting in the back of the church at her funeral and looking up at you in the front with your dad, and the way you looked... I thought it was both the saddest and the most honest I'd ever seen you be."

Every impulse I had told me to get away. He knew too much, more than I had ever imagined he could possibly know, and the weight of his knowing was as heavy as cinder blocks on my rib cage. But why did it have to be? Why did knowing have to mean hurting? I suddenly wondered: What had I ever been around Porter besides happy? Even with my best friend in the hospital, with the worst kind of sickness looming over the town we lived in, with the remnants of another boy's violence still darkening my body—somehow, despite it all, I was safe there in his bedroom. I felt my grip on my sweatshirt loosen, felt the cinder blocks start to unpile themselves from my ribs.

"I didn't know you were there," I heard myself say, my voice a fraction of itself.

"You never knew I was there. All along."

Porter lifted his hands to gently grip my shoulders. I didn't pull away or flinch at his touch.

"Now you know. Now, maybe you can let me be there the way I've wanted to be."

I nodded. Porter nodded back, his hands still gentle on my arms. I let go of my sweatshirt entirely and was again bare in front of him, but his eyes stayed on mine.

"Wyatt," he started, lifting one hand to the back of my neck. "I'm so sorry. For all of it. For everything that's happened to you. And I'm sorry you believed that you deserved any of it. I don't care if there really is some kind of…sickness in this town. That doesn't make this"—he lightly touched a bruise along my collarbone—"an okay thing for him to do to you. It doesn't make it okay that he lied to you over and over again. It doesn't give him an excuse to keep you for himself, to use you as some kind of punching bag. You're a person, Wyatt. You're a person. You matter. And fuck, I am so goddamn sorry about the party. And I'm so sorry about Quinn."

At the mention of Quinn's name, another wave of fresh tears

surfaced, and I was a heap of crying girl in his arms again. And he let me be that.

I lifted my head from Porter's shoulder, pulling back until our cheeks brushed, lips an inch apart, and I caught his mouth in a kiss, my hands going to either side of his face. He returned my kiss with just as much urgency, but skill kept his hands careful on my body. I felt his fingertips and palms move gingerly onto my back, and I pushed my body flush against his, offering him whatever his hands could reach. It was the way I knew how to show him how I felt, to give him my body like an offering. So when Porter gently broke our kiss and put space between our lips, I was confused.

"We don't have to," he told me softly, eyes searching mine.

I must have looked as confused as I felt. He tucked a loose lock of hair behind my ear.

"You don't owe me anything."

Before I could say anything, Porter took the sweatshirt from my lap and helped me pull it back over my head and down over my bare torso. Once I was redressed, we moved up against the pillows, and I laid my head against his chest, and he held me, and we tangled our legs together, using each other as tethers to solid ground.

And just as I was about to let myself fall asleep, my body desperate for rest, I sat upright, pulse rocketing like I'd just dreamed of falling and had suddenly hit the ground.

"Porter," I gasped, grabbing handfuls of his shirt and gently shaking him.

He looked startled, hands reaching for me.

"Wyatt—"

"The cameras."

Porter seemed to stop breathing.

"The fucking cameras."

19.

It felt like my life was just some kind of dark, rejected Nancy Drew novel, and I wished it didn't. But I could have wished out loud for normalcy until I was blue from lack of breath, and it wouldn't have mattered. No matter how white-bread anyone might think their life is, everyone's is somewhere on the spectrum of fucked up. Not every mystery can be solved as easily as unmasking the villain. Sometimes, the villain isn't just one person. Sometimes, the villain is in everyone.

I considered, for a moment, a stranger from another town making it their purpose to destroy my life. I imagined this faceless person breaking into my house and killing my mother, then lying in wait for me to feel a semblance of happiness again, only to set fire to it.

It felt as plausible an answer as any, at that point. The world felt so upside down, I was ready to accept any explanation if it meant turning right side up again.

The fire had devoured the cameras themselves, but Porter still had access to the footage through an online account. The cops had assumed the footage was lost in the flames and hadn't thought to ask if the cameras had been uploading the video online. Porter rushed to his desk to pull up the video footage from the cloud, and I huddled beside him, chewing on my thumbnail. As he fast-forwarded through the hours of footage the cameras had captured leading up to the party, I paced slowly behind his chair, consulting the film reel in my mind. I played and replayed it with different outcomes, the fire starting with crossed wires, or a forgotten cigarette, or a poorly aimed confetti popper, or that faceless person taking a lighter to my entire world.

As of that morning, when they'd let us leave the station, the cops seemed ready to rule the fire an accident. But something was making me doubt that, whether it was my aching, jaded belief that I could never have anything good or my unwavering obsession with the sickness. I thought of Quinn on the ground as the smoke thickened, burning my lungs. I felt her blood on my hands. Warm, wet.

A flash of my mother's face. A bloody fist gripping a kitchen knife.

A faceless stranger—Mr. Vaughn? Some drifter?—coming down the stairs in my house.

Cash, holding his silver lighter in a white-knuckled grip at the edge of the bluff, eyes black.

I felt every inch of me bristle.

Cash wore the role too well. The violence in him had become too tangible, too real. He'd started to wear it on his skin like a battle scar, like a tattoo of serpents and wolves. He'd been so sure I was making it up, our sickness, but since he'd found his mother in the bathtub, cut open and hand still clutched around the razor, he'd become the sickest of us all. It had claimed him unrightfully, the same way he'd claimed me when he'd left his mark and taken everything else. And no matter how much I'd tried to *fix* him, to stitch up his wounds with an endless barrage of unreturned love and devotion, he never got better. His cracks only spread wider, until he was hardly whole anymore.

"Okay, this is when the party started."

I hurried back to Porter's side, resting my palms on the desk as he slowed down the video speed on the computer screen. The party materialized from four different angles, people spilling in through the open barn doors, the whole place glittering and bathed in soft colored light. Watching it this way was somewhere between uncomfortable and terrifying, like strapping into the seat of a roller coaster, knowing full well the speed and sharp curves that were to come.

Porter clicked again, and the video slowed to normal speed just as Quinn, he, and I emerged through the barn doors. I wanted to reach out, touch her, tell her to run. To get out while she could. I turned away from the screen, pulled my sleeve over my hand, and wiped away the new tears falling down my cheeks just at the sight of her on the screen. I felt like I was walking toward a cliff, prepared to jump but still terrified of landing.

When I turned back around to face the screen, Porter was approaching me through the crowd. The song we'd danced to came softly through the computer speakers, and it felt like the soundtrack to the last seconds of whatever semblance of normalcy I'd begun to rebuild for myself.

"Fuck."

Porter hit pause and rewound the video a few seconds. I watched myself twirl out of his hold, then back in again as he hit play.

"If this wasn't some freak accident, you can't tell. There's nothing here."

I followed Porter's fingertip to the far right corner of the screen, where I could just barely make out Quinn's silver-blond hair. Porter clicked through the three other views of the barn, and in each of them, the small door in the far corner was obscured by bodies and shadows. Someone could have gotten in unnoticed. Or maybe they hadn't come in at all and had set the fire from outside.

We were so focused on searching the screen for glimpses of anyone unfamiliar that the sound of screams made us both back away from the computer, our breaths catching. The sound of the ceiling beam falling cracked through the speakers before Porter muted the sound, but I'd already turned my back again, holding my elbows tightly. Porter cursed under his breath, searching every angle for an explanation.

I heard him sigh.

"Maybe the cops will see something we can't," he decided, closing the window and turning in his desk chair to face me.

"Give them this footage, and it will sit in an evidence carton in a storage room, and nothing will ever be done about this."

I was startled by the sharp snap of my own words. I faced Porter and unfolded my arms, only to fold them again, frustrated.

"They didn't do shit about my mom, Porter. They took their goddamn pictures and made their stupid statements, and then they put it all in boxes and forgot about it. About her."

"So, what are you saying?" He watched me, and I could tell he was being particularly careful with his words, like any wrong syllable could send me spiraling. "What do we do? It really could have just been an accident, Wyatt. All those wires and lights. The generators."

"And what if it wasn't an accident?" I quickly countered, half frantic. "I have to know for sure."

I bit my bottom lip. I thought of the bodies that had piled up since last November—Kristen, my mother, now possibly Quinn—and of the wreckage left behind, both literal and figurative. The twisted metal of Kristen's truck, the blood streaked down the walls in the upstairs hallway of my house, Quinn's blond hair flecked with red. Lauren McClain, poisoned by her own mother in the second grade. Jacob Feldman, who got hold of his dad's pistol in the seventh grade and acciden- tally shot his best friend, Brandon Carter. And all the other wreckage—all those bodies pulled out of the river over the years, the gunshots, freak accidents, and bloodshed. The new suspect in my mom's murder, faceless and hungry to hurt someone. Our town's cemetery had steadily become the most crowded place within the city limits.

All that violence left behind more than bodies, though, something less tangible but possibly more damaging: embers, now growing into thick, hot flames deep down in the center of me. I felt them inch up from below my lungs and up into my throat as I stood there in Porter's bedroom, staring at him, searching for the right words to tell him I thought we should burn the whole place to the ground, just like Cash had said that day up on Lawson's Bluff. He'd been right about that one thing.

I sat impatiently in front of my laptop, waiting for Jennifer's call. I'd been so anxious to talk to her, to tell her about the fire, to hear from someone who believed me about everything. She'd sent me a few more articles since we'd last spoken, mostly scans of old newspapers from the 1990s detailing more random deaths in Wolf Ridge, mostly in November. It seemed like she was really seeing the pattern, putting all the pieces together better than anyone right there in Wolf Ridge. Maybe it was willful ignorance, some belief that if we ignored what was happening, it wasn't real. Or maybe it was an active effort to cover it all up, to gaslight people like me who called it out, to make us feel crazy.

Finally, Jennifer's video call popped up on my screen. I

quickly answered and watched her materialize, her dark curls pulled up, glasses on top of her head. She offered me a terse smile, her face less warm than I remembered it being the last time we spoke.

"Wyatt," she started, a pen already in her hand, "did you get my emails?"

I nodded, wringing my hands, already getting overwhelmed thinking about everything that had happened since our last video call.

"Yeah, I did—you see it, right? It can't just be nothing. It can't."

"I see *something*, yeah." She nodded, her tone careful. "What do *you* see?"

"It's this town. Right? It must be."

I knew I sounded frantic, but I couldn't help it. I hadn't properly slept in a few days, and I could still smell smoke. Flames still flashed behind my eyes every time I shut them.

"It very well could be," Jennifer said after a beat of silence, like she'd been waiting for me to keep going. She tapped her pen, watching me. "What do you remember about the day your mom was killed?"

I'd been asked this same question a hundred times before by the cops, but it still made me bristle. Still made my insides twist into a tight knot. For a long time, I'd thought it was just grief, but now I wondered if it was something else.

"I only remember finding her. Walking in, seeing...seeing the blood. I wasn't home before that."

Jennifer scrawled something on the pad in front of her while I spoke.

"Where were you?"

"I was with…" I stopped, shaking my head a little. "Does it matter? What does that have to do with all the stuff going on in this town? I wanted to tell you about the fire—"

"The fire?" The sudden interest in her voice was enough to make me lose my train of thought for a moment, and she looked at me through the screen, expectant. "What fire?"

"Last night. We threw a party at this barn outside town, and the barn burned down. My…my best friend, she got hurt, she's really hurt. The cops say it was probably an accident, but I don't know if I believe that."

Jennifer scribbled frantically, jotting down notes the whole time I was talking. She looked up when I stopped.

"And why don't you believe it?"

I looked at her, confusion on my face. "Because," I said, simply. "This town. Nothing's an accident here. That's what I've been telling you."

"Right," she confirmed with a nod. "The sickness. You, uh…you have an interesting, plausible theory there. Tell me more about it."

The way she was agreeing with me suddenly felt less validating than condescending. It felt like a rock was sinking through my chest when I realized maybe she didn't really believe me. That she was just another person trying to placate me.

The sharp realization made me want to shutter myself

back up, made me wish I'd never opened my doors to begin with.

"I have to go," I lied, shaking my head. "I'm sorry."

An irritated look came over Jennifer's face, and I saw her start to protest as I closed out the call and shut my laptop.

A flash of anger rushed through me—every day felt more and more like screaming in the middle of a crowded room as everyone ignored me. Cash and I smiled from a picture frame beside my laptop, and I swiped it off the desk with a crash. My body sank from my chair to the floor in a pile of quiet sobs, and I cried into my palms, still seeing flames behind my eyes.

Monday marked one year since my mother's death.

The first few weeks after she died, the cops had insisted it was likely a botched home invasion, that someone had broken in expecting the house to be empty and found her instead. The first suspect they named was a guy from three counties over, but he was quickly cleared. Next, they named a drifter who turned out to have been in jail the night of her murder. I remembered sitting in the police station, nursing paper cups of hot chocolate while the police asked me what I remembered about that night. If I remembered anything new. Was the door unlocked? Were there footprints in the snow outside? Did I hear anything?

I told them the same story each time until I couldn't anymore. Until I threw up in the trash can beside the sheriff's desk during one visit to the station and my dad found that cigarette burn on the inside of my arm the next day. He asked the sheriff to stop calling us in, to stop asking me the same questions over and over. He was afraid I'd be the next body to be carried out of our house.

And in the months since, I'd convinced myself of three things: that our town was infected with a sickness that made us hungry to hurt people; that someone from Wolf Ridge had murdered my mother; and that I was doomed to replay the memory I had of that night over and over, never to learn the missing pieces of that dark, gruesome fable.

As if the month wasn't already enough of a flaming car wreck, the gray that washed over our house on the morning of the anniversary of Mom's death added another layer of pain we barely had the strength to carry. I couldn't decide what would be worse: staying in the house with the ghosts all day, or going out into town and risking *oh, I'm so sorry* interactions that would inevitably hurt more than no one feeling sorry at all. For all the sorriness that existed in our town, there sure as hell wasn't much shit getting done about the things that made us all so sorry.

Dad was waiting for me when I came downstairs. We were both already dressed, and we stood there in the foyer looking at each other, neither knowing what to say—there was both too much to say and nothing to say at all.

"You wanna take a drive?" Dad asked.

I nodded. We took our coats from the hooks by the door, and I followed him out. The sky was the same shade of gray we were trying to leave behind in the house. It followed us down Wicker, onto Getty, down to the Parkway. The heater in Dad's car hummed softly, chatter from the radio just barely audible. We didn't speak. I'm not sure we needed to.

We drove past the turnoff for the barn, still blocked with a police barricade. We went past the open gates of Porter's subdivision, over the old bridge that crossed the river. I'd figured out where we were headed when I'd noticed the small bouquet of pink lilies Dad had carried out of the house, so when he turned off the Parkway onto a dirt road, I knew we were almost there. The cemetery materialized over a hill as we rounded a corner beside a tree line. It was small, only a few acres wide, the snow-speckled ground punctuated with headstones and small mausoleums, silk flowers dotting the landscape with sudden bursts of soft color. A viewing gallery of so many Novembers.

Dad parked the car on the dirt path, and we got out. He carried the lilies in one hand and reached for mine with the other. I didn't often hold my father's hand anymore—maybe I was still in that phase between childhood and adulthood where you're strangely adverse to too much outward affection for your parents—but as we walked through the rows of stones, it was more that I *needed* his hand than anything else. Holding it felt like a silent reminder that despite where we were, despite the heaviness that shrouded our lives, we still had each other. Our broken, fucked-up little family may have been weak, may have been shitty or messy, but at least it still existed. It still mattered and still kept us safe when we needed it to.

There was a black granite stone near the far-right corner of the cemetery. We walked toward it together, hardly needing to double-check our path, mostly on autopilot. Dad knew the way better than I did, but it wasn't something I could easily forget, despite not coming here as often as I knew I should.

We stepped around the front of the stone when we reached it, and I leaned into my dad's side. Dad had chosen the black granite so the white of the engraving stood out, highlighting the stark lettering of the name we both knew better than our own heartbeats. We stood there for a while in a silence that felt neither awkward nor like it needed to be filled.

Part of me wondered if Dad was talking to her in his head. More of me knew he was.

I thought of a little over a year ago, a week or so before Mom had died. I'd stood halfway up the steps, screaming at my mother, who stood at the bottom. She'd only asked where I'd been, and I'd exploded into a rage, maple whiskey still on my tongue. I'd never understood before why she was always so intent on pulling me away from Cash. But now, I wondered how much of myself I'd still have left if I'd just listened to her.

Dad finally stepped forward and set the lilies down. Then he moved back and wound his arm around my shoulders, keeping me tight against his side.

"She hated roses," he started, even though he knew I knew the story. I didn't mind hearing it again.

"I got them for her on one of our first dates, and she just gave me this...face."

I could hear him smiling, just a little.

"So I asked her what her favorite flower was, and she told me to guess. I got her a different kind of flower each time I saw her from then on, and when I got her lilies, I knew from the smile she gave me when I handed them to her that I'd finally gotten it right."

I let him tell the story because stories were all we had now. I stood against his side and listened to him recount what was steadily becoming the mythology of my mother, this woman who had lived in our house but was starting to feel more like a friend we once knew and were starting to forget. I could practically *feel* Dad grasping to hold on to every last bit of her. But his hands were as slippery as anyone else's. No one can ever really hold memory tight enough to last.

I tried the hardest to hold on to the warmest pieces of my mother—her worn-out purple robe and how she'd wrap me in it with her; that messy bun she wore on days she was off work; the way she and my dad teased one another, still so in love. But it was always the sharpest pieces that seemed to linger the longest. Our vicious fights, all teeth and claws. The swift slam of my bedroom door. The look on her face when she dug through all my jacket pockets and found crumpled cigarettes, a lighter, and a prescription bottle filled with weed. And the way my voice broke the last time I told her I wished she was dead.

My mother was the sad ending of a fable, meant to teach me something about being human. But there I was, still trying to pick apart the details and change the story.

When we got home, Dad kept the TV volume louder than

usual, the sounds of a cooking show marathon partially drowning out the deafening silence that had settled on the house. Up in my room, I opened my laptop, checking to see if Jennifer had emailed again after I'd cut our call short. Some part of me still hoped she held some kind of answer, some kind of doorway to finding peace. Quieting the ghosts. I wanted her to indulge me again, to treat me like I wasn't just some sad motherless girl grasping for reasons why bad things happened.

There was an email, short and curt:

Wyatt—

I'm sorry that you're struggling to understand what happened to your mother. After the research I've done, it looks most like a string of bad luck. Crime rates often spike in the colder months, so it isn't unusual that your town sees more of it at the end of the year. There is no reason to believe a sickness is responsible for these events. I learned from my Detroit homicide beat that people really are capable of the absolute worst things, whether we like it or not.

I'd really like to talk with you more about your mother. Don't hesitate to reach out.

—J

I slammed my laptop closed and shoved it across my bed.

I put my headphones on to block out the sounds of the ghosts crying and laughing and screaming in the hallway.

The school hallways rattled like empty cages come Tuesday morning.

Dad tried to convince me to stay home like I did on Monday, but after two days in the house with the ghosts, we were both about ready to shed our own skins.

The hallways weren't loud enough to drown out the whispers about the fire and Quinn tucked behind open locker doors, the unvoiced but somehow still oppressive *sorriness* everyone from Wolf Ridge was so good at. Some girls huddled and cried. Boys stood stoic, hands loose at their sides, once again practicing how to carry their own bodies in the wake of another potential loss they would all inevitably forget about eventually.

Losing came as easily as breathing to us. We were the children of loss, of suicides, of car wrecks, of massacres. Tragedy was our rite of passage. We wore our personal body counts like war medals. Swapped stories of slit wrists and sudden heart attacks and twisted metal like trading cards.

I was almost to my locker when I stopped short, the air suddenly leaving every cubic inch of space in the hallway.

The chipping blue paint of my locker was covered in copies of the same image, haphazardly and angrily stuck to the door in disarray—a picture of Porter, Quinn, and me taken the night of the party, overlaid with bright red text: *YOU DID THIS.*

Everything stuttered into slow motion. People moving around me in the hallway were suddenly just shadows and whispers. The air refused to return. I felt as if I was drowning, trying to pull breath into my lungs but finding only water.

The embers asleep in my veins ignited. I crossed to my locker, the air coming back all at once, just to feed the kindling in my chest. Echoes of screams played on a relentless loop in my mind as I ripped the papers from my locker. Once it was bare down to its old blue paint again, I whipped around to find that everyone in the hall really had stopped moving to watch me and the shredded paper at my feet.

"What the fuck do you want?" I heard my own voice, but I felt separate from it, somehow.

Before I could scream anything else, arms wound around me.

Porter held onto me, tightened his grip when I struggled against him, lungs burning and fists clenched, ready to combust at any moment.

"The hell are you all looking at?" he snapped at the people still watching me like I was a caged animal. They began to disperse, leaving behind their anxious whispers and the sounds of slamming locker doors and hurried footsteps on the polished floor.

"We've gotta get you out of here." Porter's voice came from above my head. I was buried against his body. I could barely form a coherent thought before it caught on fire inside of me.

By the time the second bell rang, we were outside, a rush of cold air filling my burning lungs as the noise woke me from the spell I'd fallen under. Porter still had his arm around me, carrying the weight I couldn't, both physical and otherwise. I let him. I needed him to bear some of the load so I could use what energy I had left to try and calm the flames before they consumed me. Before they consumed the whole fucking town.

And then I saw him.

Leaning against the side of his truck, smoking a cigarette, watching Porter and me as we walked out to the lot together.

My steps slowed. An iciness I thought I'd left behind in his bedroom suddenly prickled over the back of my neck. Porter slowed alongside me, not noticing Cash until he followed my gaze, which was fixed, locked, and loaded on him.

"Wyatt..." Porter started, tightening his hold on me, but I was already pushing him back. He tried to snatch my hand, but I smacked his away.

I felt the hard thud of my shoes on the pavement in my ears. As I got closer, I saw Cash's face change, watched him drop his cigarette and stub it out with the toe of his shoe. He opened his mouth, likely poised to offer me some kind of bullshit, but before he could say anything, my open palm connected with the side of his face with a sharp crack of skin on skin. His head whipped to the side, jaw slack, hair falling into his eyes at the impact. It was the first time we'd touched since he'd hurt me, and it still didn't feel as icy as I needed it to. I felt my heart beating in my throat, my hands shaking with adrenaline as I watched him, waiting for a reaction, waiting for him to say something, anything. Waiting for him to try and speak so I could tell him to shut the fuck up, that it was *my* turn to talk and his to listen.

I could feel Porter a few yards behind me, frozen in place,

and I wondered if part of him was brimming with the same satisfaction I was right then.

"I know it was you," I practically spat at him. "What the fuck are you trying to do?"

Cash slowly turned his head to look at me. He lifted one hand to his cheek, gently adjusting his jaw and pushing his hair back out of his face.

I clenched my fist, dug my nails into my palm, ready to pull back and hit him again if he so much as moved one inch closer to me. Porter stayed behind me, gave me the space I needed, but his presence alone served to douse some of the raging wildfire inside my chest.

"How fucked up do you have to be to think you are some kind of martyr in all this?"

She was back—the girl with the razor blades under her skin, the one who was all cuss words and cigarettes. Diamond tough.

"I bought your bullshit for so long. I let you make me feel crazy for thinking something was wrong with the people in this town, but now I know you were just trying to keep me from noticing that you're the most fucked of them all."

I heard Porter take in a breath behind me. Cash was stoic, stone-faced, taking it.

"And I fucking know about you and Kristen."

At the mention of her name, Cash's face suddenly changed, a shift so sharp it cut into me. He looked pained, his eyes strangely softened, and he blinked quickly, like he'd just felt the sting of oncoming tears. He looked, all at once, grown and small. Hurt and grief reduced even him to shards.

"Then you must know what *he* did," Cash said finally, nodding toward Porter. "That *he's* the reason she's dead. He took those photos because he knew she wanted me and not him. *He* made her do it."

"He"—I gestured in Porter's direction—"didn't do anything. Kristen did it to herself, Cash. She killed herself. And maybe it was this town, or maybe it was because she couldn't look at herself in the mirror anymore after sleeping with you. I know I can't."

Whatever sickness lived inside Wolf Ridge, it darkened Cash's eyes right then. I felt it stirring inside my own chest, fanning the flames, telling me *hit him hurt him ruin him.* But I clenched my fists tight at my sides, nails pressing so hard into my palms that I was sure I was drawing blood.

"Did you ever think maybe there's another reason why you can't look at yourself in the mirror, Wyatt?" Cash's voice was edged with desperation.

There was something in his face, in his voice, in the words he spoke that made the film reel in my head jump harshly backward, queuing up frames spattered with red—the hallway, the carpet, my open, shaking hands. I closed my eyes against what felt like a hard shove to my chest, but when I opened them, I saw that no one had touched me. Porter was still hovering behind me, Cash still a few inches out of arm's reach, that haunted, knowing look still on his face.

I wanted to draw back and hit him again. I wanted to swing and keep swinging until I felt the warmth of blood—mine or his, either would have satiated me. But I steadied myself with a full breath in. I stepped slowly backward, putting more space between Cash and me, almost afraid of what might happen if I didn't, like the darkness he was carrying would somehow seep into the ground we were sharing and twist itself around my ankles. Cash just watched me, body poised to jump back, the black of his eyes glittering in the gray morning light. I could have sworn he looked afraid of me.

When I finally willed myself to turn my back to him and start walking in the opposite direction, I could still feel his eyes on me, following my every step, his gaze like a thick, sharp hook right between my shoulders.

20.

Porter parked the Jeep a few miles outside the town after turning off on a dirt road that led down to a pond. In the twenty or so minutes since we'd left the school parking lot, I'd replayed the images in my head a thousand times—the ones Cash's words had called to the forefront of my memory, all of them red and angry and broken, like the film had been cut and pieces stolen. I grasped around inside my own head, desperate to uncover the lost frames and see the whole picture.

What had he meant by *another reason* for not being able to look at myself in the mirror? And why had his question, and the way his voice had sounded when he asked it, wound itself around every available bit of space in my mind?

In the driver's seat beside me, Porter was quiet. He didn't rush to fill the silence. We both sat there in it, my pulse finally slowing. After a few minutes, he picked up his phone from the cup holder. A moment passed before music filled the space around us, settling against our bodies, filling up our lungs when we breathed in. I didn't recognize the song, but I didn't really need to know it in order to feel it. To let it sink in through my skin and wrap around every snapped heartstring.

The sharp edges in my head went dull. The half moons I'd dug into my palms no longer stung. I dropped my head back against my seat, shut my eyes, and listened. I let the sound, rather than Cash's words, fill up the space in my mind. I suddenly wanted to go to bed, wanted to curl up under my covers and sleep until the first of December.

"Why don't we go see Quinn?" Porter said. He was already putting the Jeep in reverse, twisting around in his seat to back out onto the road again. He let the song play out, and I curled and uncurled my fingers like a fighter unclenching after a match. And then his hand was reaching for mine, and I let him take it, let him slide his fingers between mine, press our palms together.

This boy. This ghost. This memory I'd forgotten I had. I remembered his smile from across the classroom when I came back to school after my mom died, the only one who dared make eye contact with me, unafraid to catch the heaviness I was carrying around with me.

Outside, rain had started to fall. The windshield wipers swished quietly under the sound of the music—another song that felt like sinking, another melody I could lean into, lean on.

Something sad but hopeful, like Porter seemed right then, his grip on my hand tightening once or twice as he drove.

The hospital was a good fifteen-minute drive from the pond. In the time it took to get there, we didn't speak at all, and that felt okay.

The beam had hit Quinn hard enough to cause bleeding in her brain, and smoke had burned her lungs. When we got to the hospital and made our way to her room, a machine was still pumping air into her, breathing for her. Porter gave me space, let me go to her side and sink into the chair next to her bed. I noticed the sweater draped over the back of it—her mother's. I wondered where she was, if she'd gone home to sleep or if she'd simply dissolved into thin air like so many other mothers in our town. Crushed under the weight of grief, of the potential for things to get even worse than they already were.

And for a second, I thought of my own mother, a flash of a memory—me, standing halfway up the steps in our house, screaming at her where she stood in the foyer, weed and liquor on my breath, that I'd rather she die than keep me away from Cash.

A nurse appeared on the opposite side of Quinn's bed, startling me back into that moment, where I landed hard, even my bones hurting when I realized all over again that it was real. All of it. The nurse checked the numbers on one of the beeping monitors, jotted something down, then offered me her best, saddest prepackaged sympathy smile. She was young. The name badge clipped to her lilac scrubs read EMILY. She had a loose ponytail gathered at the back of her neck, and her fingernails were painted a light blue. She could have been my mom at twenty-something. She could have been anyone's mom right then, though, with that look on her face.

"Um," I started, clearing my throat to find my voice. "Can you tell me what's…" But I lost my words, instead just looking down at Quinn, then back up at Emily the nurse, hoping she'd fill in my blanks. Porter stood stoically by the door, watching.

Emily hugged Quinn's file to her chest. Gave me another one of those smiles.

"Your friend got hurt pretty bad," she started, and I fought the urge to wave her off and tell her never mind, that I didn't need her bottled response, fed to me like I was some sad child. But I just took Quinn's hand. Curled my fingers around her still ones.

"The doctors stopped the bleeding and swelling, but her lungs were badly damaged from the smoke, so the machine is here until she gets a little stronger and doesn't need help breathing on her own. But she's pretty lucky. Her burns are mostly minor. Had she stayed in there even a few more moments…" She trailed off, then pressed her lips together in a thin smile. "Probably shouldn't have told you all that, but her mom mentioned you might come by. She's going to be okay. Your friend is really lucky. Kind of a miracle, you know."

One more pasted-on smile, and she turned on the toes of her lace-ups and hurried out of the room, still clutching the chart against her chest. My eyes followed her out, then fell on

Porter, still standing by the door, arms crossed loosely over his chest. He looked anxious, like every muscle in his body was tense under his skin, bones steadily stiffening the longer he stood in the room. He must have felt my eyes on him, because I saw him try his best to loosen his tight limbs, tucking his hands into his pockets.

"My dad was sick last year," Porter said after a moment. "I haven't really been here since then."

In my mind, I added another tick mark to the list of wrongs our town had committed. I wanted to know what he'd been sick with, if he had looked as helpless as Quinn did right then, if that image still haunted Porter, even though his dad was upright and better now. If he still thought about what it might've been like to lose him. If he'd seen his father in a hospital bed and pictured him in a coffin instead.

But I just nodded. I didn't speak. I picked up Quinn's bandaged hand in both of my own and kissed the back of it, then set it gently back down on the bed, tucked neatly against her side. I got up, stepped around the end of the bed, and Porter lifted his hand and offered it to me. Every bit of me wanted to take it, to find safety in it, to let the room stop spinning once our fingers wound together. But just as his fingertips met mine, Quinn's mother appeared in the doorway, a paper coffee cup in one hand and a startled look on her face. I dropped my hand back to my side. I didn't know why, but it suddenly felt like the three of us were standing on the deck of a sinking ship with only one life vest, trying to decide who deserved it most.

And before I could tell her I wanted her to have it, wanted her to be the one who made it out alive, she wound me up in her arms. She hugged me tight against her, and I could smell what was left of her perfume, the same kind Quinn and I used to steal spritzes from in middle school, a scent that had come to be the only one I associated with *mother* anymore. This mother, the one who'd driven me home in the middle of the night in fifth grade when I got scared at a sleepover and wanted my mom. The one who never forgot my birthday and who always brought Quinn and me smoothies after school on Friday afternoons in middle school. I realized right then, in the arms of a woman who didn't *have* to love me but did, that I was starting to forget my own mother, more and more every day.

How did she smell? When was the last time she'd held me like that? I thought of the time I'd screamed at her that I wished she'd die—how she held me after all the times I'd shouted something just as sharp. She always welcomed me back like a guilt-heavy parishioner looking to confess. Did she ever stop forgiving me?

I couldn't remember. I held on to this woman, this stand-in mother, grasped handfuls of the back of her sweater, but really I was grasping for something else—pieces of a person I was losing. Someone I had maybe already lost.

On the walk out to the parking lot, my phone dinged with a search alert. I'd put one on any mentions of my mother or the town. The new article had been posted to Jennifer Scolitz's website.

Daughter of Murdered Woman Blames Urban Legend for Mother's Death

I felt something inside me ice over. My jaw set, and I felt Porter's eyes on me as we walked.

"You okay?" came his voice from beside me.

I pocketed my phone and nodded, straightening my shoulders.

"Let's just go home."

I fell asleep on the short ride back into Wolf Ridge. The inside of my head felt thick with pins and needles, the kind that sting your limbs when they fall asleep from lack of circulation, but I couldn't shake this sleep away. It lingered and lingered. It held on to me the way Porter seemed to be trying to, like he was afraid I was about to float away at any moment.

School wouldn't be over for a few more hours, but Porter didn't drive us back there. He took us to his house instead, and when he parked the Jeep in the driveway, the feeling of his hand gently squeezing mine woke me.

The basement was quiet and bathed in shadows from the pale light coming through the narrow windows along the top of the far wall. Porter flipped a switch, and the gas fireplace came on, but he still grabbed a blanket from the back of the sectional to pull over us once we'd collapsed into the corner of it. Porter let me tuck my body into his side, let me settle against him like a current—he didn't care if I eroded him. He let me fall back asleep against him, let my body have the rest those weeks had been stealing from me.

I opened my eyes, and I was standing in the doorway of my house, snow blowing in around my feet from outside. A record was playing on Mom's old Victrola—a looped chorus I couldn't make out the words of. I felt the cold biting from the open door behind me. My head felt like it might leave my shoulders and float away. My ears rang. The music skipped in and out. I was in my socks, and my feet felt wet. Had I walked through the snow without shoes?

I curled my fingers into my palms. Felt something sticky. Wet. Warm.

When I looked at the floor, it seemed to tilt upward.

The scuffed wood floor of our foyer was patterned in footprints, red and smeared, running between the door and the bottom of the stairs. The carpet on the steps was stained red all the way up to the top, where the stairs disappeared into the dark hallway.

Everything's edges were blurred. Loose. Moving. Nothing was holding its shape.

This—this was the missing piece of the film reel. These were the frames I'd lost.

I lifted my hands to look at them. Found them soaked in sticky red, just like my clothes, just like my socks. I looked around frantically, trying to gather as many of the pieces as I could, desperate to know what I'd lost, what details had been missing all those months.

The sound of my heartbeat in my ears and my own ragged breaths drowned out the music.

I wanted to move, to rush up the stairs, to find my mother, but my feet seemed cemented in place. There was a knot forming in the center of me. I felt dizzy and unsteady. Every sound was in a minor key, sickening and unsettling, pieces of a song I knew but didn't recognize anymore.

And then a body was coming down the stairs.

A set of long legs emerged from the darkness at the top, clad in jeans, wet with blood. A wet red fist gripping the handle of a kitchen knife. A white T-shirt, soaked through. The familiar curves of elbows and arms, the shoulders I slept against in the bed of the truck on warmer afternoons.

But before that face came into view like a swift stab to my gut, I was back on Lawson's Bluff a few weeks before, watching the same hand that had just held the knife flick open a lighter and hold it out over the town, ready to set it all ablaze.

"Would be messy," came his voice from beside me. "Maybe too messy."

And I was picturing it—Porter Dawes, his insides on the outside. Never once wondering how I'd conjured the image so easily, how I'd painted the bloody portrait in a just few quick strokes.

The paintbrush hadn't been imagination.

It had been memory.

It was raining harder by the time I reached the end of Porter's driveway. I could hear him behind me, calling my name, trying to coax me back into the house, but the rain picked up and started to drown him out. It was cold enough that the rain stung my face, bit at my hands, started to chill me as it soaked through my sweatshirt. But I barely noticed. I was running it all through my head, this new version of a story I'd thought I knew every bit of, this memory I hadn't realized I had. It felt like trying to shove together puzzle pieces that didn't fit. Square peg, round hole. Nothing was making coherent sense, even as it played in a continuous loop in my mind, finally a complete whole that I wished I could put through a mental shredder. I didn't want it. I didn't want these new pieces. I didn't want to know what had really happened. After a year of wishing I had answers, suddenly all I wanted was to forget them. To go back to not knowing.

This was why Cash had tried so hard to convince me our sickness wasn't real. This was why he had tried to convince me to stop digging, why he'd turned so pale when he'd told me the police had a new suspect. He'd been worried that suspect was him.

I was in the middle of Porter's street when his fingers caught my wrist. His touch yanked me back down to earth, the volume coming back on all at once, rain coming down harder and louder, drenching me straight through my clothes. And when the sound came back, I realized Porter was yelling over the noise, his hands grabbing my shoulders. I remembered standing in the middle of the barn just like that, searching for his voice like it was miles away even though his face was inches from mine. He was always trying to save me. I was always too far gone.

His mouth was shaping words like *get out of the street* and *what is going on*, and I was shaking my head, dizzy and frantic and wet, shrugging out of his grasp.

"Cash," I heard my voice say, but I hardly recognized the word in my mouth. It felt sharp. It tasted of metal and ash.

"What?" Porter shook his head, grabbing for my shoulders again. "Wyatt, what about Cash?"

"My mom." I felt lead in my lungs. "It was Cash."

No matter how hard I tried, I couldn't seem to pull air in. Porter still looked confused, but his face began to change, the crease in his forehead softening, his jaw starting to go slack. He dropped his hands from my shoulders. Let us drift apart in the ocean of his street. I was shivering. He looked defeated, wet hair sticking to his forehead.

"How do you know?" he called over the rain. "How do you know it was him?"

I spiraled. I was ten feet above my own body, watching it happen.

"Because," I shouted back at him, wishing the rain was enough to rinse me clean, to wash all the blood in my memory down the street and into the gutter, "I think I was there."

21.

Last November

Cash dumped two small white pills from a tiny plastic baggie onto the glass top of the coffee table.

We were in his basement. The ice on the roads and the steady snow had left us with a day free from school, and his dad was working a few towns over, so we had the house to ourselves. The narrow basement windows let in a cold, gray light. My head was already floating a few inches above where it normally sat, thanks to the few bowl packs we'd just shared. My mouth felt thick and dry, my body ten times its normal density. I was becoming part of the old basement sofa, melting to fit into it like a flattened throw pillow.

The white pills on the coffee table shivered and twisted,

then set themselves right again. I blinked myself back to consciousness.

This was his idea. This was his afternoon, built of spent cigarette butts and a mostly empty bottle of cheap whiskey.

"You aren't going to hallucinate," he promised, offering me one of the pills. "You'll just feel good. Don't you want to feel good?"

I knew *he* wanted to feel good. I knew he had become a walking wound since his mother's death a year ago. I knew he had tried just about everything to sew himself up, but nothing stuck—his seams always came undone again. Left him exposed. Raw. Insides tumbling out. In the year since his mother had split herself open in their bathtub, Cash had dissolved into basic instincts, only ever protecting himself, only ever trying to feel good, and only ever failing at it. Falling short.

I saw his mother in his face that afternoon. That lift in his cheekbones. The purse of his lips as he carefully rolled a joint. She still inhabited him. She kept living, some part of her trapped inside his rib cage. The bad part. The sick part. The part that she'd probably been trying to bleed out of herself.

I took the pill from Cash and rolled it slowly between my fingers. At that point, I would have done anything he asked. That day in his basement, I was at the peak of my unflinching obsession, somehow convinced Cash needed me with the same intensity that I needed him. Right then, on that couch, snow piling higher against the basement windows, he could have asked me to slit my own throat.

Or maybe even someone else's.

Days before, we'd stood in the cemetery and watched them lower Kristen Daniels into the dirt. Cash and I had lingered back from the group gathered by her open grave, passing a cigarette back and forth. I didn't know it then, but his heart was shredding itself. And there we'd stood, with my thoughts wound up in him and his eyes hidden behind dark sunglasses while he watched yet another woman he loved get swallowed up by the earth because the world had been so unkind to her that the only thing she could think to do to make it all stop was to die.

I was thinking about death on that couch. While I pinched the tiny pill between my fingertips and watched Cash, I thought about how I'd kill myself if I ever did it. For a moment, my thoughts corrected *if* to *when*. Our sickness was itching at the back of my throat, ready to bloom into a full-blown fever dream of delicious violence at any moment. But it wasn't always loud, our violence. It wasn't always overt. Sometimes it swam inside our heads unnoticed, like a parasite. The drugs and the liquor kept it quiet, and we'd been turning to them more and more since Cash's mom had died, and almost constantly since Kristen's funeral. Even at school, I was only ever half sober, climbing up on the radiator in the bathroom to take hits from a joint and exhale out the frosted window.

It was safe to say that when I wasn't thinking about drugs or drinking or Cash, I was thinking about death. I reveled in it like some kind of sick form of meditation. It wasn't even like I *wanted* to die; I was just hungry for the thought of it, enough that I knew it wasn't normal teenage bullshit. Sometimes I got hungry enough that it scared me. That's when I smoked, or drank, or unwrapped myself like a broken Christmas toy for Cash. And when I came home smelling like weed and booze, my mother would be waiting for me with this look of exhaustion on her face, and she'd ask me if I felt proud of the choices I was making, and I'd spit fire at her and tell her to stay the fuck out of my life.

I don't know how much time I spent sitting there, holding that pill, thinking about how my mother being dead would make everything easier, before I finally sat up, tossed the pill into my mouth, and swallowed it down. Cash had promised it was just molly—something to calm me rather than make my pulse race—and I would have breathed in or swallowed any substance that offered that kind of promise. We were always looking for the next high, the next thing that would help us sink into that couch and disappear for hours on end. Anything that would let us leave that place, even if our bodies stayed.

I didn't remember much of what came next. The memories came in shards and pieces—sharp, sudden. I didn't remember how long we sat there before I finally spoke. And I didn't know where the words came from—maybe someplace deep in the center of me, that place I hid all the id-driven, violent thoughts I pretended not to have—but I remembered what the words were: "Sometimes, I wish my mom would die, too."

"You should tell her," he said, his lips against my ear,

weakening me even more than the drugs spreading through my system like a virus. "Let's go tell her."

Was it hours before we got to my house? Did we stay in the basement? Did I imagine the entire thing, hallucinate it, even though he promised I wouldn't? The next piece came like a record skip, knocking me ahead until I was standing in my own kitchen, watching Cash pull a knife from the block on the counter.

"I'll do it for you," he whispered, and I felt confused, my head full of sawdust, unsure if I was really standing there or not.

And then my broken film reel dropped me in the foyer, where I yelled for Cash, trying to find him. Upstairs, someone was screaming, but I couldn't figure out if the screams were coming from inside my head or not.

I looked up, and Cash was coming down the stairs, the knife from the kitchen dangling loosely from his bloody fingers. The time in between the basement and that moment was fractured, half-dissolved, but somehow we had ended up there, and I couldn't remember ever telling him *no*.

Cash had never been one to hear the word *no* and heed it. I always saw Cash so selectively, picking and choosing the parts I wanted to glorify and worship and pretending the dark parts weren't there at all.

But this wasn't a dark part I could ignore. There he was in my mind, coming down the steps, shirt smeared in thick red. Handling the knife like a trophy, looking half mad.

He got to the bottom. Crossed the foyer to where I stood. And pulled me in by the back of my neck to kiss me, like we were celebrating, like I was Bonnie and he was Clyde and now we'd get to ride into the sunset, victorious and free. But that was the moment I became the least free I'd ever been. That was the moment I became a hostage to Cash, to the sickness we shared. The madness of two.

We left the front door open when we stumbled back outside. I don't know if I really understood what had just happened or if the drugs in my veins were letting me believe none of it was real, that we were running through a fever dream together, our bodies still back on the couch in his basement. He held my hand, and we ran down Wicker Road, and Cash zipped his coat up over his blood-soaked T-shirt, and we ran all the way to the river while it snowed, far enough that my hands went numb in the cold, but the drugs tricked my body into feeling warm, fingers wound between Cash's. And we stood on the bank, and I felt dizzy while I watched him throw the knife into the water, watched it disappear beneath the surface before he swept me up in his arms and grasped a handful of my hair at the back of my neck and kissed me so hard our teeth clicked together. He kissed me like a victor, like he'd just come home from a war I'd asked him to fight for me. But I'd never asked. I hadn't wanted this. Whatever piece of me knew what had just happened was sickened, so sick it made me double over beside the river and throw up.

But the rest of me had already forgotten what he'd done. By the time we got back to his house and thawed our frozen bodies by the fireplace and he threw his bloody clothes into the flames and I watched them burn, I'd already forgotten whose blood it was. My mind had already shrouded reality to protect me, to save me from knowing I'd stood there in my foyer while Cash murdered my mother upstairs. My memory rebuilt itself while I slept on the floor of Cash's living room, the drugs wearing off in time for me to get up a few hours later and go home. To walk into the house with brand-new eyes, blank-slate innocent; to climb the stairs and step into a pool of my mother's blood; to lay eyes on what the boy I loved had done to her.

I spent a year convinced someone else had done it. I spent that year so tangled up in Cash I could barely see past him, past the place he held in my life. And all the while, he knew what he'd done, made plans to escape our tiny town for reasons other than just wanting a fresh start somewhere else. He knew what he'd done, and yet he kept stealing from me, as if my shelves could have been any emptier, as if I really had anything else for him to take.

On the couch in the basement that afternoon, passing cigarettes and the bowl back and forth, I felt weightless and filled with lead at the same time. It was a feeling that often came with being around Cash. One moment, he seemed to worship me, pressed kisses to my lips without me asking first, made me his without any effort, and the next moment, he made the inches between our bodies feel like miles. He could be light-years away and sitting right beside me.

When I'd said I wished my mother were dead, he had

seemed to appear next to me again all at once, like I'd called him back from whatever far off place he'd been in, sent the universal distress signal the people in our town seemed to answer without question. *Help me, I want to hurt someone.*

Now that I'd realized the truth, remembered the pieces I'd protected myself from, there was still a question circling in my mind—who had I really wanted to hurt? I struggled to answer that question for year-ago Wyatt, but the Wyatt who stood soaked in cold rain in the middle of Porter's street had a new answer. And she wasn't going to forget it this time.

22.

Even after I told him what we'd done, Porter didn't call the cops and turn me in. He didn't tell me to leave or call me a monster. I wondered if his comfortable life, with his very-much-alive mother and his dad who had merely been sick once, made it impossible for him to understand the unfill-able hole left by loss. Made it impossible for him to under-stand the way Cash changed after finding his mother dead, changed in a way that made murdering my mother make perfect sense to us both. Even though I'd forgotten what had happened, even though my mind had filled in the gaps with questions instead of truth, there was still a part of me that *understood*. A part that wasn't even surprised or angry or horrified to find out the truth. A part that probably knew all along but had chosen to pretend otherwise anyway, because it was easier to pretend I still had some shred of humanity left in me.

Even though I was sure he didn't totally understand and that there were still huge pieces of my story that didn't add up for him, Porter didn't send me away. He coaxed me back inside, peeled off my wet clothes, and helped me into dry ones. The scent of his sweatshirt as he pulled it over my head was almost overwhelming—a kind of safety and innocence I thought I'd just lost entirely, somehow wrapped around me again. Like I was still worthy of it. Like I could still be gifted something like warmth or closeness and it wouldn't sear my skin like holy water on a person possessed.

"Look, just because you had this dream doesn't mean you—"

I put my hand up before Porter could say anything else.

"It wasn't just the dream, Porter. I *remember* now. It's a memory. It happened. I was there."

"Okay, so you were there—you didn't *do* it. That was Cash. We need to turn him in. He has to be held accountable, Wyatt."

I shook my head, crossing to the end table by Porter's front door where he'd dropped his keys and where my phone was sitting. I picked it up, then snatched his keys up, too, throwing them to him.

"I need you to take me home. There's something I have to do."

I was already making a plan in my head—get home, find Cash. What would happen once I found him was still unclear, but I found myself thinking about the gun in Dad's bedside drawer.

"Wyatt, you can't be thinking about handling this yourself. You need to leave this up to the cops."

"Oh, 'cause they've done such a bang-up fucking job so far, Porter? How the fuck was Cash never brought in for questioning? Why did no one even think to ask us where we were? What we were doing? Why I couldn't account for almost an entire day?"

"They had no reason to think you had anything to do with it, Wyatt. You found her. I saw you in the days after that. You didn't look like someone who had any answers."

I stopped with my hand on the door, tightening my grip on the handle until my knuckles went white. I heard Porter take a slow breath in behind me.

"I think they've given up," I said, turning back to look at him. "I think they've stopped caring when people die in this town. Like it's some kind of tax we have to pay. But I'm done letting them ignore what's going on here."

I pulled the door open. Porter watched me from the middle of the foyer, keys in hand, like he wasn't sure what to do next. Like he wasn't sure if he should leave with me or put distance between himself and the train wreck of my life. He must have considered that following me could mean falling into the hole I'd spent the last year digging. He must have wondered if I was worth it—this girl who'd stood by while a boy she thought she loved had murdered her mother. He must have been wondering whether it was too late to pretend I didn't exist. To go back to his perfect, easy life, all love songs and slow dances with pretty girls and a new car every year. All white T-shirts and hair that fell just right. I was a black smudge. He could wipe himself clean of me, or he could get even dirtier. He could swim or drown.

Porter nodded slowly a few times and grabbed his jacket from the hook by the door. I followed him without a word to the Jeep. And on the way out of his neighborhood, I watched him from the passenger seat, watched his jaw set and clench. And I knew he was going to do more than follow me through whatever fire I was about to set.

He was going to help me set it.

The gray afternoon light was fading by the time we got to my house. Dad's car was missing from the driveway, but I knew he was in the city, tutoring. I practically leapt from the passenger seat and sprinted across the yard to the front door, hands fumbling with my house key.

When I opened the door, the breath in my lungs seemed to stiffen, tight in my chest. I saw Cash in my head again, coming down the steps, blade catching the light. I felt his mouth against mine, hungry and greedy, proud of what he'd done, like he was expecting me to thank him. To be grateful.

I shoved past the ghosts in the foyer and jogged up the stairs, hearing Porter close behind. Even though I knew he'd made the choice to come with me, to involve himself in the raging wildfire that was my life, part of me wanted to tell him to go home.

He followed me to my dad's room but hovered in the doorway, and I could feel his eyes on me as I rushed to the bedside table and yanked the drawer open.

"Wyatt, what are you doing?"

The gun wasn't in the drawer. I dug through it, pushing aside papers and loose old family photos, but it wasn't there. Had he hidden it? Had he somehow known I'd go looking for it? I scanned the room, half frantic, trying to think of what he might have done with it.

"I'm handling this."

I checked the junk drawer in Dad's dresser, swiped one hand under the mattress, searching for a brush of cold metal. I looked under the bed, yanked shoeboxes down from the top shelf of the closet, leaving the boxes and everything in them scattered all over the floor.

"Handling it how?"

I looked at Porter, still standing in the doorway, watching me tear apart my father's room, his face wary. I pushed up the sleeves of his sweatshirt I was wearing, my own face feeling flushed with warmth as I worked my way through the room, a tornado leaving wreckage in my wake. I stood still a moment before I hurried out of the room and shoved past Porter, jogging back down the stairs to the den. He followed me closely, hovering near me while I yanked open every drawer in my father's desk, tossing papers and books as I went.

"Wyatt," I heard Porter say, but his voice got lost in the chaos I was unleashing on the room. I shoved things off the desk, crossed to the bookshelf and knocked books to the floor as I searched for a hiding place. I needed that gun. I needed it because

I knew that without it, I'd crumble in front of Cash. I needed it so I could keep my edges from blurring when I did find him.

My phone ringing cut through the room, and I stumbled back, startled as it pulled me out of the frantic trance I'd fallen into. I took it out of the pocket of my borrowed hoodie. The name on the screen sent a sharp stab of anxiety through the center of me. "It's the sheriff."

In those few seconds as my phone rang in my hand, a thousand possibilities went through my mind. The sickness wanted me to believe the worst—they knew. Cash had pinned it on me. Had he known I'd figure it out?

I swiped my thumb over the bottom of the screen and put the phone to my ear.

"Sheriff Grant?"

"Wyatt. I have some news. I gave your Dad a call, but he didn't answer. Is he home with you?"

The edge to his voice made my heart rattle in my rib cage. I looked at Porter, taking in a slow breath before I answered.

"I'm at home. He isn't here. What's the news? News about what?"

I heard him take in a breath. "I'd like you to call your dad and then come down to the station. I can send a squad car for you."

Porter was watching me, forehead creasing in concern as the color drained from my face, as I was already filling in the blanks in my mind.

"Wyatt?" The sheriff's voice was louder now. "We found evidence of an accelerant at the barn. We believe the fire was started on purpose, and we have reason to believe Cash Peters was involved."

Even though I'd already believed it, having it confirmed felt like swallowing razor blades. I closed my eyes and went back to that night in the barn, the flames climbing the walls and the screams sharp in my ears, Quinn's crumpled, bleeding body on the ground. And then I went back to the night in Cash's bed, where I was hollowed out—the night I shed my own skin and came out a jagged, unrecognizable version of myself.

A heat rose in the center of me that I hadn't felt before, an anger I couldn't swallow back, couldn't quickly silence. If there was a sickness, it was feeding on me, replicating inside me, the pieces that made me up built out of madness, out of a growing hunger to hurt someone. To hurt the person who had hurt me. The sickest one of all of us. Patient zero.

"Yeah, yeah, I understand," I said, interrupting the sheriff as he repeated that he wanted me at the station for further questioning.

"Once you get hold of your Dad, call me—"

"Yes, okay. I've gotta go."

He was still talking when I ended the call, a stiff silence collecting in the space between Porter and me. He watched me, waiting for me to explain what was happening and why the color had drained so quickly from my face. But in that moment, I was somewhere else. I was trying to figure out where Cash might be and how I could get to him before the cops did. It wasn't enough for him to be arrested. Someone needed to stop him before he could hurt anyone else.

I went back to tearing the den apart, grabbing a box off of one of the shelves. A small luggage lock hung from the latch. I jiggled it a few times, but when it didn't budge, I crossed to the desk and smashed the lock against the corner of it, sending Porter staggering back toward the doorway.

"Wyatt, what the fuck are you doing?" he shouted.

I tossed the broken lock aside and set the box on the desk. I could feel Porter's eyes fixed on me, burning the side of my face as I opened the lid and let out a breath. There was the gun, alongside a box of bullets. I reached in and picked it up, the weight of it familiar in my hand from those few times my dad had taken me to the gun range. Had taught me how to use it.

"Wyatt..." Porter spoke my name through a breath. "I really hope this isn't what you meant when you said you were handling it."

I checked the magazine. It was loaded. Porter's breathing hitched as I slid the safety off and clicked it back on again.

Everything stilled.

It felt like I was moving in slow motion as I tucked the gun into my hoodie pocket and walked out of the den, leaving the mess I'd made, the eerily silent aftermath of a storm. I hardly cared if Porter followed me at that point; I actually hoped he wouldn't. I didn't want this blood to be on his hands. Because I knew as I walked out the front door into the rain that there would be blood. I knew that where I was going, there was no coming back.

23.

I tried to gather up whatever good pieces of Cash were left in my mind.

My instinct was to think only of mornings in his passenger seat, afternoons in the bed of his truck, sharing breaths and touches. Of grade school, when we ate ice cream by the lake, his hair still so blond it caught the summer sunlight. Watching him grow up from the little boy I played with on the playground into the teenager with that sweet, low voice who picked me up in his old truck, and who made me feel like the only person in the universe when we were alone together. For all his coldness, for all his hesitancy to love freely, Cash was so *easy* for me to love. I'd built my world around him, starting when we were children, and even now, I was still running to save him from himself.

All I knew was forgiving him. Loving him in spite of every-thing. I remembered cradling him in my arms like a broken child after his mother's death, helping him change his clothes and keeping him hidden in my bed for days when he was too scared to set foot in his own house. I remembered seeing him like that—shattered, raw, all the hidden pieces of him suddenly like unlocked doors I was finally allowed through. He had emptied himself out to me in those days, let me see him in shreds, let me handle him like glass and help him glue his pieces back together in some semblance of what they used to be.

He had let me have so much of him that when he went back into hiding, put his walls back up stronger than before, I had those pieces to hold on to, to remember that version of him by. And that was the version I was sure loved me—the Cash who made me grilled cheese and white chocolate milkshakes at Watson's and drove me out to the water when he knew I needed to get out of our suffocating town, the Cash who stood in the snow with me in short sleeves and kissed me. I could still feel his smile against my lips.

How could *that* Cash be the same Cash who had lied to me day after day, let me love him when his heart was with someone else, who had *killed* my mother and then let me go on hurting and drowning in all my unanswered questions? There were two versions of him, two different people, and I didn't like who one of them was. I didn't know that person. And that person needed to be stopped before he could hurt anyone else—himself included.

Porter coaxed me into his passenger seat, insisting on coming with me despite me begging him to stay out of it.

"I'm pretty sure we're way past that," he said as he turned the key in the ignition.

We drove toward Cash's house. I needed to see if he was there, to see if the police had already found him. I kept my hand on the gun in the pocket of my sweatshirt, fingers wound tight around the cold metal, and I could feel Porter's eyes flashing over at me as he drove, like I was a lit fuse he was worried might go off without warning.

"Stop, stop, stop. Stop here." I sat forward in my seat as we turned onto Cash's street. I could see his house, his driveway full of police cruisers. His truck was missing.

Porter gripped the steering wheel as we watched a few deputies emerge from the front door, empty-handed.

"He's not there," I breathed, my pulse spiking.

"Where would he go?" Porter had his eyes fixed on the cops. If they looked up the street, they'd see the Jeep. They'd know it was Porter.

Porter Dawes, the person in Wolf Ridge Cash seemed to hate the most. I thought of weeks before, standing on the bluff, watching Cash hold his lighter out over our sick town, listening to him muse about killing Porter.

"I know where he is." I looked at Porter. "Let's get out of here before they see your car."

Porter put the Jeep in reverse and backed out onto Getty Street. I pointed toward the north end of town, and he followed my direction without asking any questions. I wondered if he was too afraid or if he just didn't want to know what was going on in my head. I didn't blame him. It was dark in there, a mess of storm clouds and debris. It was a hurricane I wouldn't want to get swept up in, either, if I had a choice.

Porter got to the split between the back road up to the bluff and the highway and looked to me. I nodded toward the bluff, my stomach backflipping. Porter's eyes lingered on me for a moment that felt like an hour as we sat at the fork, the Jeep's right blinker clicking in an eerie rhythm with the windshield wipers.

It was a few miles' drive up the mountain to the bluff. A ride that normally lasted a handful of minutes seemed to stretch into a daylong journey, the rain picking back up as the Jeep followed the curves of the dirt road up to the top. As we came around the last bend, I saw Cash's truck. My fingers tightened around the grip of the gun in my sweatshirt.

What if I had this all wrong? What if the story I'd stumbled upon was just another version of the nightmares I'd been having for a year, another fragment of pain splitting off inside me and manifesting into something darker?

I thought of Cash. The arms I'd found safety in for years. The way he'd wrap them around me from behind and let me slide my cold hands into his jacket pockets while we stood by the water. The deep, sweet laugh that I hadn't heard in earnest since his mother had died. The way I'd watched each and every one of his threads come undone in the years since, popping like violin strings, sharp enough to draw blood with their snap. I tried to map his descent into this vicious, angry version of himself. Remembered all the months I'd spent blaming Wolf Ridge, pointing fingers, but never pointing one at him, even when I *knew* he was, at any given moment, a grenade with the pin pulled.

The faces of every suspect the police or I had investigated in the last year flicked through my mind like a lineup. Was it really one of them? One of those strangers? Had somebody come into Wolf Ridge just to feed on us? Or had it been someone from Wolf Ridge all along, like I'd always thought? Patient zero. The sickest of us all. But the one I'd trusted the most.

Past the blockade, I could just make out Cash's form through the rain, standing near the edge of the bluff. In my head, images of all the times I'd stood right there with him sharing joints and cigarettes were overlaid with flickers of him walking down the steps, wearing my mother's blood. Porter put the Jeep in park behind Cash's truck, and by the time he reached for the emergency brake, I was already out of the car, his voice shouting my name getting lost under the sound of the rain as I walked toward the blockade.

The closer I got to Cash, the harder I waged war inside of myself, torn between firing at his back and falling to my knees in front of him, begging him to tell me why he'd done it. He turned as I ducked under the blockade, wet hair stuck to his forehead, eyes fraught with a kind of pleading I'd never seen him wear. He wore that desperation like an ill-fitting coat. I wanted to rip it off of him. After what he'd done, he didn't deserve to look so helpless and lost.

"I knew you'd find me," he said over the rain, and I stopped where I was, leaving some distance between us, half afraid to bridge it, half afraid of how badly I wanted to.

"I know what you did, Cash."

The waver in my voice threw my pulse into overdrive. I didn't want him to see me breaking. I couldn't let him.

He just nodded a few times, and I watched him with a growing sickness in my stomach.

"Don't you mean what *we* did, Wyatt?"

I was clenching my teeth hard enough to send a flash of pain through my jaw. I curled my fingers around the gun in my sweatshirt, thumbing the safety.

"I didn't—"

"Who do you think I did it for?"

The air left my lungs in a sharp breath. I gasped, his words like a rope around my throat, tightening as he took a few slow steps toward me.

"I did it because you needed me to. I tried to tell you what happened—I tried to talk to you about it—but you didn't remember, so I just fucking played along. *Protected* you from it. I couldn't bring myself to admit to it; I knew you'd be wrecked. And you spent the whole last year so fixated on what happened when it was right in front of you. I knew you wouldn't find the answer and knew it was safer to let you blame something else. Someone else."

The rain was coming down in steady sheets, loud enough that I didn't hear Porter coming up behind me, just saw Cash's expression change from that desperate, pained look to anger in a matter of seconds.

"Guess we're all murderers here, aren't we, Dawes?" Cash shouted over the rain, his eyes fixed on Porter. "Since you're the reason she drove her truck off this bluff. She was gonna get out of here. We both were. We weren't going to become a piece of the fucking scenery here like you two—"

"Cash, shut the fuck up!" I heard myself scream, but I felt separate from the sound, felt like I was hovering ten feet above it all, watching, not participating.

"What, Wy? You can blame your fucking sickness for wanting your own mother dead, but you can't blame it for making your precious Porter do what he did to Kristen? There is no sickness, Wyatt. Some of us are just born broken. And even if there is a sickness? It isn't just here in Wolf Ridge. It's in everyone. Every single person is capable of doing what I did. Some are just better at hiding it."

Cash sounded so broken, his voice edged with the threat of tears. I hadn't seen him so ripped open since his mom had died. He looked even more desperate now, a convict on death row making a final plea.

"Wyatt." Porter's voice came from behind me. "This isn't worth it. Let's get out of here."

But that heat I'd felt burning in the center of me had gone from matchstick to wildfire in the time I'd spent standing there in front of Cash, that driving rain seeming to wash away any bit of forgiveness I had left.

"Yeah, Wyatt," Cash chided, his voice like a fistful of thumbtacks. "Get out of here. Run away. Go back to believing you're innocent, that I'm the only monster standing here right now."

I shook my head, but I felt Porter's hand curl around my arm, felt him start to pull gently, carefully, like he was coaxing a wild animal. But I had my eyes fixed on Cash, and he was staring right back, like he was daring me to stay there and show him exactly what I'd come for.

"Let's go," Porter urged, but I yanked my arm away from him. Cash almost looked pleased to see me standing there, in the midst of unraveling. But his features were shadowed in desperation.

"Go on," he said again, this time with an edge in his voice that sent me back a few steps. "Run away."

"No." I had the gun out of my sweatshirt pocket and pointed at Cash before he could open his mouth to say anything else. I heard Porter curse behind me, but Cash barely faltered. He stared at me, at the gun pointed at his face, as blank-faced as if he were looking at his own reflection. I thought, for a moment, that maybe he was.

"Tell me why. I need to know why you did it. Why you killed my mom. I want answers. You owe me that much."

Cash's jaw set. I could hear my heart beating in my ears, the rain just white noise filling up the space between our bodies. The longer I stared at him, the more I felt like I was somewhere else—his basement, the back of his truck, my seat at the counter at Watson's, the places I used to consider the safest. While I waited for him to speak, I felt each one build itself around us, then watched each one dissolve into ash.

"You think that's all I did?" Cash finally said. "Kill her?"

I felt a stab of ice right in the center of my chest. "The fire."

"And the vigil," he added, his words clipped. "I told you already, didn't I, Wyatt? Every time you brought up that sickness you swore was making all of us kill ourselves and each other? Every single time, what did I tell you?"

I was already shaking my head before he finished talking, replaying every scene of us on the bleachers, passing cheap liquor between us while I tried and failed to put together all the broken pieces in my mind, while I tried and failed to keep Cash's attention on me rather than whatever bottle he was drowning in.

"No," I argued, adjusting my grip on the gun, keeping it pointed straight at him. "That's bullshit, Cash—"

"Is it? Why is it so hard for you to believe that people are just *bad*, Wyatt? Oh, I know—because then you'd have to accept the fact that *you're* just bad. That *you* set your own mother's death in motion. That *you* aren't innocent. That you've been crying for a year over something you did to yourself."

I didn't want to listen anymore. I didn't want to hear him blaming me. But I wasn't sure if it was because I didn't believe him or because I did. Because believing him meant I was the monster I swore I'd never let myself become.

"You didn't have to grow up in this town to turn into this, Wyatt. Neither did I. Neither did Kristen, or anyone else who has contributed to the body count. This is in our DNA, not our zip code. No matter where you go, you're always gonna be this broken."

My throat burned and tightened, heat rising up from my chest. If Cash wanted me to believe I was broken, then I would. I would be broken, irreparable, so caught up in my own darkness that I wouldn't even notice if I pulled that trigger. At least one of us would be out of our misery. At least one of us wouldn't be able to hurt anyone else.

But even a broken, smashed-to-shards me couldn't do it. Even the Wyatt with the sharp edges. Cuss words, cigarettes, diamond tough. Even *she* wanted to spare Cash.

I lowered the gun to my side and clicked the safety back on.

Cash looked an inch from breaking. His eyes widened and narrowed again.

"What—suddenly don't have it in you?" he said, baiting me.

I'd almost forgotten Porter was still behind me until I felt him reach for the gun, inching it out of my loosened grip until I let go of it entirely. I never took my eyes away from Cash.

"Why'd you start the fire?" I asked, defeat dripping from my voice, and I wished I could bring myself to sound stronger, to not let him know he'd succeeded in breaking me down. "What was hurting Quinn and endangering everyone else supposed to accomplish?"

"I didn't—" He cut himself, losing his voice, pushing a

hand through his wet hair anxiously. "Quinn getting hurt was an accident. I..." His voice broke again, and a fist clenched tight in the center of me, his pain cutting through me. "It was supposed to be you and me. Everyone else was getting in the way. I went there for you. You were getting away, Wyatt. I wasn't just trying to set fire to your stupid fucking party. I wanted to burn down everything in the way. You needed to see that it was all just smoke and mirrors. It just got fucking out of hand, all of it."

It felt surreal, listening to him confirm every worst fear I'd had. Everything felt like dripping clocks and that eerie state of not-quite-awakeness, when all the worst dreams happened, overlaying reality. I couldn't wake from this one. No matter how hard the rain came down, no matter how cold I got, shivering hard enough that my knees wanted to buckle, I couldn't wake up. I flashed back to Cash's bed the night he tried to take me when I didn't want to be taken, thought of the way I'd memorized the outline of the fist-shaped crack in his bedroom wall, counted his breaths until he'd finally left. I thought of how even then, I hadn't felt as hollowed out as I did standing there on the bluff, faced with the truth I'd been fighting for months—that everyone, no matter how *good* they were, was capable of darkness. Kindness, empathy, gentleness—they weren't hardwired, they were chosen. And as much as I wanted to choose *not* to let Cash live, as much as I wanted to pull that trigger, I was realizing it wouldn't matter. The world, with or without Cash in it, was going to keep turning. Those of us who were left would keep hurting, keep suffering, keep taking our pain out on the people around us regardless of whether Cash was alive to see it happen.

If there was a sickness, I wanted to stop letting it win. I wanted to choose right, for once.

"The cops are gonna find you," I told him, thinking he may not hear my softened voice over the rain. "And you're gonna pay for everything you did."

"Not as much as you will."

I stiffened. Felt my hand twitch, wishing my fingers were still wrapped around the gun. Without it, I felt like that sad, spineless version of myself that always melted into the ground in front of Cash, took on the shape of whatever he needed me to be. Edgeless. Weak.

"You're gonna pay more than anyone, Wyatt. You're gonna have to live the rest of your life knowing what you did, what you let happen. And don't think for *one second* that I won't tell the cops. If I'm going down, I'm taking you with me. Hell, I'll take him too." He pointed to Porter.

"We all deserve to be ruined," Cash went on, half mad, pushing his wet hair back again and pulling on it desperately. "Him. Me. *All* of us."

The next few seconds unfolded in slow motion. It felt like it was happening outside of reality, a waking. Dripping clocks. The in-between feeling of being both asleep and awake.

In a few strides, Porter stepped out in front of me and crossed to where Cash stood. In the time it took me to pull in a breath, Porter's hands were gripping Cash's jacket, shoving hard against his chest, sending him stumbling backward. I watched from somewhere outside myself, half expecting to wake up at any moment, to notice the rain was falling from the ground instead of the sky, but it just kept coming down. I kept not waking up.

Porter and Cash were caught in a tangle of limbs and hard blows, the rain drowning out their sounds as they fought. A year of believing he'd been responsible for Kristen's death bubbled up and reduced Porter to the violence we were all built from. The fire that sat in the center of us like pilot lights, waiting to be ignited.

Their scuffle came to a head, Porter pushing Cash's chest again, shoving him away hard. The breath in my lungs turned to lead as I watched Cash step backward to catch himself, his foot finding only empty air. The instant it took for him to disappear over the edge of the bluff went on for hours, like I was trapped in some cruel, sick time warp, forcing me to watch it happen over and over until we caught back up to speed. Until suddenly, it was just Porter and me and the rain and nothing else.

My legs carried me involuntarily to Porter's side as he stood on the edge, looking down. He threw his arm out in front of me to keep me from going too far, but he never lifted his eyes from where they were fixed—on Cash, an inhuman pile of contorted limbs on the rock at least a hundred feet below. The rain blurred the outlines of his broken body, but I could still see it, even when I closed my eyes.

Wake up, Wyatt, I screamed inside my head, so loud I was sure Porter could hear it.

Sirens were building in the distance. The police must have figured out where Cash was hiding out.

"I told them."

Porter's voice cut through the white noise of the rain, startling me.

"I texted your dad our location from your phone when you got out of the car."

He was calm, his face expressionless. He wiped his bloody nose on his sweatshirt sleeve, looking over the edge of the bluff.

"It was you or him," he said, his voice icier than the rain hitting our faces.

And we stood there at the edge, our broken town spread out in front of us, wearing our newest burden like chains around our necks as the sirens climbed the bluff behind us, bathing us in blue and red.

Epilogue

"**This morning on News 8, the teenager who took his own life** by jumping off a bluff in Lamoille County last week reportedly confessed to last year's brutal murder of Lydia Green, forty-two, before his death. Police have confirmed the teen's involvement in the homicide—"

Dad shut off the TV and tossed the remote onto the couch.

"You don't have to go today, Wyatt," he said, though I was already throwing my backpack over one shoulder.

"I'm fine, Dad. I wanna go."

"You've only got a few days before break. You could just get a jump start on it."

"I've had a jump start—I've been sitting in this house for almost a week. I need to get out of here and be around other humans before I lose my mind."

He studied me, skeptical. I studied him back, narrowing my eyes, waiting for a smile to split his face. When it did, I gave him one back, hoping it was convincing enough for him to believe.

"All right. But if you change your mind—"

"I won't. Come on, we're gonna be late. I've gotta make up a calc quiz before first period."

Dad spent most of the short ride to school watching me out of the corner of his eye. It had been nearly a week of him eyeing me like I was a lit firework, a week of eggshells, a week of making sure my bedroom door was always unlocked in case the nightmares came back. To him, I must have seemed like cracked glass—just about anything could cause me to shatter. But to me, those cracks were just reminders of my newfound freedom, one that hadn't come for free but that he'd never know the real price of. It was easier if he didn't.

I had barely unbuckled my seatbelt before Porter jogged up to hold the car door open. He watched me skeptically while he helped me shoulder my backpack and shut the door behind me.

"You sure you're ready?" he asked quietly, his hand gentle on my arm. "We could just go to my house and watch weird foreign documentaries and overdose on Chinese food."

I shook my head. Muscle memory wanted me to pull away, to put space between our bodies. But in this new life, in this new version of me, I didn't have to do that. The only voice I had to listen to anymore was my own. And this girl—she didn't need to be diamond tough. Sharp. She just had to be Wyatt.

"We're here, so let's stay. I'm ready," I assured him, feeling Dad's eyes on us from the other side of the car as he shouldered his bag and locked the doors. He was stalling, watching me like a patient on a locked ward, but I knew he was trying his best to give me space. To let me process things in my own way. He gave us one more long glance before he started off toward the school.

"He's...never gonna trust me, is he?" Porter said, watching my dad over my shoulder. I turned to look and saw Dad fall in with a few other teachers on the way inside the building. When I turned back to Porter, I just shook my head.

"No. Probably not."

Porter forced a weak smile, hooking his arm around my shoulders as we headed across the parking lot.

"Yeah, well... I guess that adds up."

I heard his words, but suddenly, I wasn't listening. My eyes were on the parking spot a few yards away, where an old sea-green Ford truck was parked. A boy in black jeans and a leather jacket over his hoodie leaned against the driver's side door, rolling a cigarette between his fingers. He tossed his hair out of his eyes as I passed and smiled at me. I could taste maple whiskey in my mouth. Smelled cedarwood and bergamot.

But I blinked, and the parking spot was empty. Just an oil stain left on the pavement.

"Hey, you okay?"

Porter's voice was a rope thrown to me in rough waters. I pulled myself back in. Put my feet back on land.

"Yeah. I'm okay."

And as I said it, I tried to decide if I was lying or if I'd really convinced myself it was true. As we walked inside, I decided it could be.

At least for a while.

There were still some time left in November, after all.

Acknowledgments

This book was a wild journey from start to finish, and it wouldn't have been possible without the constant support and encouragement from my incredible agent, Sharon. I am so grateful for her tireless belief in me and my work. Annie and my powerhouse editing team at Sourcebooks held my hand through this process and made it so, so wonderful. It is such a privilege to work with these folks and to be on this amazing imprint. Thank you for making a lifelong dream come true.

To Katelyn–my best reader, my forever first set of eyes, my favorite reviewer. You are the strings that hold up this silly heart.

To the absolutely phenomenal folks I got to live and write and learn with at two residencies at Vermont Studio Center, and to the little winter town that shaped this book—thank you, thank you, thank you. I will never forget reading the first page of this novel while standing with you all on the bridge in negative wind chills and snow. And a warm, huge thanks to the artists and friends at the Fish Factory Creative Center of Stöðvarfjörður in Iceland, where I wrote the final chapters and then promptly ran up the hill beside the fjord and took a gigantic breath of relief.

Mom, Dad, Michael, Christopher, Catherine, Danielle—I await your book reports. Oh, and I love you. Joseph and Jackson, I'll save you some copies for when you're old enough to read the f-word.

Thank you, thank you, thank you.

About the Author

Photo © Vito Grippi and Lizz Dawson

Sara Walters works as an advocate for victims and survivors of domestic and sexual violence in central Pennsylvania. She previously worked as a reproductive rights advocate and a college instructor. She earned her MFA in creative writing at the University of South Florida and studied children's and young adult literature while earning her doctorate in education at the University of Tennessee. She believes in the power of storytelling as a voice for survivors and aims to give space to the stories too often silenced.

FIREreads

— $\circledS$ **#getbooklit** —

Your hub for the hottest young adult books!

Visit us online and sign up for our
newsletter at FIREreads.com

@sourcebooksfire

sourcebooksfire

firereads.tumblr.com